FEAR   HUMOUR   FANTASY

From the imagination of Damon Knight comes another volume of stories that plunge vividly into other worlds, other dimensions, other times.

The story of George, a rather endearing alien who liked being punished.

A doorway that will take you anywhere—except back to earth.

A terrifying meeting between man and alien that ends in horror.

Tales that range from the bizarre to the grimly humorous, each one an invention of a brilliantly original mind.

DAMON KNIGHT

IN DEEP

MAGNUM BOOKS
Methuen Paperbacks Ltd

A Magnum Book

IN DEEP
ISBN 0 417 02220 4

First published in Great Britain 1964
by Victor Gollancz Ltd

First paperback edition 1966 by Corgi
Magnum edition published 1978

Copyright © 1963 by Damon Knight

Magnum Books are published by
Methuen Paperbacks Ltd
11 New Fetter Lane, London EC4P 4EE

Made and printed in Great Britain by
Richard Clay (The Chaucer Press) Ltd
Bungay, Suffolk

ACKNOWLEDGMENTS

'Four In One' published in *Galaxy Science Fiction*
Copyright © 1953, by Galaxy Publishing Corp.

'An Eye for a What?' published in *Galaxy Science Fiction*
Copyright © 1957, by Galaxy Publishing Corp.

'Stranger Station' published in *The Magazine of Fantasy
and Science Fiction*
Copyright © 1956, by Fantasy House, Inc.

'Ask Me Anything' published in *Galaxy Science Fiction*
Copyright © 1951, by World Editions Inc.

'The Country of the Kind' published in *The Magazine of
Fantasy and Science Fiction*
Copyright © 1955, by Fantasy House, Inc.

'Ticket to Anywhere' published in *Galaxy Science Fiction*
Copyright © 1952, by Galaxy Publishing Corp.

'Beachcomber' published in *Imagination*
Copyright © 1952, by Greenleaf Publishing Company

CONTENTS

FOUR IN ONE

I

GEORGE MEISTER had once seen the nervous system of a man —a display specimen, achieved by coating the smallest of the fibers until they were coarse enough to be seen, then dissolving all the unwanted tissue and replacing it with clear plastic. A marvellous job; that fellow on Torkas III had done it—what was his name? At any rate: having seen the specimen, Meister knew approximately what he himself must look like at the present moment.

Of course, there were distortions: for example, he was almost certain that the neurons between his visual center and his eyes had produced themselves by at least thirty centimeters. Also, no doubt, the system as a whole was curled up and spread out rather oddly, since the musculature it had originally controlled was gone; and he had noticed certain other changes which might or might not be reflected by gross structural differences. The fact remained that he—all that he could still call *himself*—was nothing more than a brain, a pair of eyes, a spinal cord and a spray of neurons.

George closed his eyes for a second. It was a thing he had learned to do only recently, and he was proud of it. That first long period, when he had had no control whatever, had been very bad. He had decided later that the paralysis had been due to the lingering effects of some anaesthetic—the agent, whatever it was, that had kept him unconscious while his body was being—— Well.

Either that, or the neuron branches had simply not yet knitted firmly in their new positions. Perhaps he could verify one or the other supposition at some future time. But at first, when he had only been able to see and not to move, knowing nothing beyond the moment when he had fallen face first into that mottled green and brown puddle of gelatin ... that had been upsetting.

He wondered how the others were taking it. There were others, he knew, because occasionally he would feel a sudden acute pain down where his legs belonged, and at the same instant the motion of the landscape would stop with a jerk. That could only be some other brain, trapped like his, trying to move their common body in another direction.

Usually the pain stopped immediately, and George could go on sending messages down to the nerve endings which had formerly belonged to his fingers and toes, and the gelatinous body would keep on creeping slowly forward. When the pains continued, there was nothing to do but to stop moving until the other brain quit—in which case George would feel like an unwilling passenger in a very slow vehicle—or try to alter his own movements to coincide, or at least produce a vector with the other brain's.

He wondered who else had fallen in—Vivian Bellis? Major Gumbs? Miss McCarty? Or all three of them? There ought to be some way of finding out.

He tried looking down once more, and was rewarded with a blurry view of a long, narrow strip of mottled green and brown, moving very slowly forward along the dry stream bed they had been crossing for the last hour or more. Twigs and shreds of dry vegetable matter were stuck to the dusty, translucent surface.

He was improving; the last time, he had only been able to see the thinnest possible edge of his new body.

When he looked up again, the far edge of the stream bed was perceptibly closer. There was a cluster of stiff-looking, dark-brown vegetable shoots just beyond, on the rocky shoulder; George was aiming slightly to the left of it. It had been a plant very much like the one that he'd been reaching for when he lost his balance and got himself into this condition. He might as well have a good look at it, anyhow.

The plant would probably turn out to be of little interest. It would be out of all reason to expect every new life form to be a startling novelty; and George was convinced that he had already stumbled into the most interesting organism on this planet.

Something *meisterii*, he thought. He had not settled on a

species name—he would have to learn more about it before he decided—but *meisterii* certainly. It was his discovery, and nobody could take it away from him. Or—unhappily—him away from it.

It was a really lovely organism, though. Primitive—less structure of its own than a jellyfish, and only on a planet with light surface gravity, like this one, could it ever have hauled itself up out of the sea. No brain, no nervous system at all, apparently. But it had the perfect survival mechanism. It simply let its rivals develop highly organised nervous tissue, sat in one place (looking exactly like a deposit of leaves and other clutter) until one of them fell into it, and then took all the benefit.

It wasn't parasitism, either; it was a true symbiosis, on a higher level than any other planet, so far as George knew, had ever developed. The captive brain was nourished by the captor; wherefore it served the captive's interest to move the captor toward food and away from danger. *You steer me, I feed you.* It was fair.

They were close to the plant now, almost touching it. George inspected it; as he had thought, it was a common grass type, of no particular interest.

Now his body was tilting itself up a ridge he knew to be low, although from his eye level it looked tremendous. He climbed it laboriously and found himself looking down into still another gully. This could go on, no doubt, indefinitely. The question was, did he have any choice?

He looked at the shadows cast by the low-hanging sun. He was heading approximately northwest, or directly away from the encampment. He was only a few hundred meters away; even at a crawl, he could make the distance easily enough ... if he turned back.

He felt uneasy at the thought, and didn't know why. Then it struck him that his appearance was not obviously that of a human being in distress; the chances were that he looked rather more like the monster which had eaten and partially digested one or more people.

If he crawled into camp in his present condition, it was a certainty that he would be shot at before any questions were asked, and only a minor possibility that narcotic gas would be used instead of a machine rifle.

No, he decided, he was on the right course. The idea was to get away from camp so that he wouldn't be found by the relief party which was probably searching for him now. Get away, bury himself in the forest and study his new body: find out how it worked and what he could do with it, whether there actually were others in it with him, and if so, if there was any way of opening communications with them.

It would take a long time, he thought, but he could do it.

Limply, like a puddle of mush oozing over the edge of a tablecloth, George started down into the gully.

The circumstances leading up to George's fall into the something *meisterii* were, briefly as follows:

Until as late as the mid-twenty-first century, a game invented by the ancient Japanese was still played by millions in the eastern hemisphere of Terra. The game was called *go*. Although its rules were almost childishly simple, its strategy included more permutations and was more difficult to master than that of chess.

Go was played, at the height of its development—just before the geological catastrophe that wiped out most of its devotees—on a board with nine hundred shallow holes, using small pill-shaped counters. At each turn, one of the two players placed a counter on the board, wherever he chose, the object being to capture as much territory as possible by surrounding it completely.

There were no other rules; and yet it had taken the Japanese almost a thousand years to work up to that thirty-by-thirty board, adding perhaps one rank and file per century. A hundred years was not too long to explore all the possibilities of that additional rank and file.

At the time George Meister fell in to the gelatinous green-and-brown monster, toward the end of the twenty-third century A.D., a kind of *go* was being played in a three-dimensional field which contained more than ten billion positions. The galaxy was the board, the positions were star systems, men were the counters. The loser's penalty was annihilation.

The galaxy was in the process of being colonised by two

opposing federations. In the early stages of this conflict, planets had been raided, bombs dropped, and a few battles had even been fought by fleets of spaceships. Later that haphazard sort of warfare became impossible. Robot fighters, carrying enough armament to blow each other into dust, were produced in trillions. In the space around the outer stars of a cluster belonging to one side or the other, they swarmed like minnows.

Within such a screen, planets were utterly safe from attack and from any interference with their commerce ... unless the enemy succeeded in colonising enough of the circumambient star systems to set up and maintain a second screen outside the first. It was *go*, played for desperate stakes and under impossible conditions.

Everyone was in a hurry; everyone's ancestors for seven generations had been in a hurry. You got your education in a speeded-up, capsulised form. You mated early and bred frantically. And if you were assigned to an advance ecological team, as George was, you had to work without any decent preparation.

The sensible, the obvious thing to do in opening up a new planet with unknown life forms would have been to begin with at least ten years of immunological study conducted from the inside of a sealed station. After the worst bacteria and viruses had been licked, you might proceed to a little cautious field work and exploration. Finally—total elapsed time fifty years, say—the colonists would be shipped in.

There simply wasn't that much time.

Five hours after the landing, Meister's team had unloaded fabricators and set up barracks enough to house its two thousand, six hundred and twenty-eight members. An hour after that, Meister, Gumbs, Bellis and McCarty started out across the level cinder and ash left by the transport's tail jets to the nearest living vegetation, six hundred meters away. They were to trace a spiral path outward from the camp site to a distance of a thousand meters, and then return with their specimens —providing nothing too large and hungry to be stopped by a machine rifle had previously eaten them.

Meister, the biologist, was hung with collecting boxes to the point that his slender torso was totally invisible. Major Gumbs had a survival kit, binoculars and a machine rifle. Vivian Bellis, who knew exactly as much mineralogy as had been contained in the three-month course prescribed for her rating, and no more, carried a light rifle, a hammer and a specimen sack. Miss McCarty—no one knew her first name—had no scientific function. She was the group's Loyalty Monitor. She wore two squat pistols and a bandolier bristling with cartridges. Her only job was to blow the cranium off any team member caught using an unauthorised communicator, or in any other way behaving oddly.

All of them were heavily gloved and booted, and their heads were covered by globular helmets, sealed to their tunic collars. They breathed through filtered respirators, so finely meshed that—in theory—nothing larger than an oxygen molecule could get through.

On their second circuit of the camp, they had struck a low ridge and a series of short, steep gullies, most of them choked with the dusty-brown stalks of dead vegetation. As they started down into one of these, George, who was third in line—Gumbs leading, then Bellis, and McCarty behind George—stepped out onto a protruding slab of stone to examine a cluster of plant stalks rooted on its far side.

His weight was only a little more than twenty kilograms on this planet, and the slab looked as if it were firmly cemented into the wall of the gully. Just the same, he felt it shift under him as soon as his weight was fully on it. He felt himself falling, shouted, and caught a flashing glimpse of Gumbs and Bellis, standing as if caught by a high-speed camera. He heard a rattling of stones as he went by. Then he saw what looked like a shabby blanket of leaves and dirt floating toward him, and he remembered thinking, *It looks like a soft landing, anyhow.* ... That was all, until he woke up feeling as if he had been prematurely buried, with no part of him alive but his eyes.

Much later, his frantic efforts to move had resulted in the first fractional success. From then on, his field of vision had moved fairly steadily forward, perhaps a meter in every fifty minutes, not counting the times when someone else's efforts had interfered with his own.

14

His conviction that nothing remained of the old George Meister except a nervous system was not supported by observation, but the evidence was regrettably strong. To begin with, the anaesthesia of the first hours had worn off, but his body was not reporting the position of the torso, head and four limbs he had formerly owned. He had, instead, a vague impression of being flattened and spread out over an enormous area. When he tried to move his fingers and toes, the response he got was so multiplied that he felt like a centipede. He had no sense of cramped muscles, such as would normally be expected after a long period of paralysis: and he was not breathing. Yet his brain was evidently being well supplied with food and oxygen; he felt clear-headed, at ease and healthy.

He wasn't hungry, either, although he had been using energy steadily for a long time. There were, he thought, two possible reasons for that, depending on how you looked at it ... one, that he wasn't hungry because he no longer had any stomach lining to contract; two, that he wasn't hungry because the organism he was riding in had been well nourished by the superfluous tissues George had contributed....

Two hours later, when the sun was setting, it began to rain. George saw the big, slow-falling drops and felt their dull impacts on his 'skin.' He did not know whether rain would do him any damage or not, rather thought not, but crawled under a bush with large, fringed leaves just to be on the safe side. When the rain stopped it was dark, and he decided he might as well stay where he was until morning. He did not feel tired, and it occurred to him to wonder whether he still needed to sleep. He composed himself as well as he could to wait for the answer.

He was still wakeful after a long time had passed, but had made no progress toward deciding whether this answered the question or prevented it from being answered, when he saw a pair of dim lights coming slowly and erratically toward him.

George watched them with an attentiveness compounded of professional interest and apprehension. Gradually, as they came closer, he made out that the lights were attached to long,

thin stalks which grew from an ambiguous shape below—
either light organs, like those of some deep-sea fish, or simply
luminescent eyes.

George noted a feeling of tension in himself which seemed
to suggest that adrenalin or an equivalent was being released
somewhere in his system. He promised himself to follow this
lead at the first possible moment; meanwhile he had a more
urgent problem to consider. Was this approaching organism
the kind which the something *meisterii* ate, or the kind which
devoured the something *meisterii*? If the latter, what would he
do about it?

For the present, at any rate, sitting where he was seemed to
be indicated. The body he inhabited made use of camouflage
in its normal, and untenanted state, and was not equipped for
speed. So George held still and watched, keeping his eyes half
closed, while he considered the possible nature of the approaching animal.

The fact that it was nocturnal, he told himself, meant nothing. Moths were nocturnal; so were bats—no, the devil with
bats, they were carnivores.... The light-bearing creature came
nearer, and George saw the faint gleam of a pair of long,
narrow eyes below the two stalks.

Then the creature opened its mouth.

It had a great many teeth.

George found himself crammed into some kind of crevice in
a wall of rock, without any clear recollection of how he had got
there. He remembered a flurry of branches as the creature
sprang at him, and a moment's furious pain, and then nothing
but vague, starlit glimpses of leaves and earth.

The thing was impossible. How had he got away?

He puzzled over it until dawn came, and then, looking down
at himself, he saw something that had not been there before.
Under the smooth edge of gelatinous flesh three or four projections of some kind were visible. It struck George that his
sensation of contact with the stone underneath him had
changed, too: he seemed to be standing on a number of tiny
points instead of lying flat.

He flexed one of the projections experimentally, then thrust
it out straight ahead of him. It was a lumpy, single-jointed

caricature of a finger—or a leg.

George lay still for a long time and thought about it with as much coherence as he could muster. Then he waggled the thing again. It was there, and so were all the others, as solid and real as the rest of him.

He moved forward experimentally, sending the same messages down to his finger-and-toe nerve ends as before. His body lurched out of the cranny with a swiftness that very nearly tumbled him down over the edge of a minor precipice.

Where he had crawled like a snail before, he now scuttled like an insect.

But how.... No doubt, in his terror when the thing with the teeth attacked, he had unconsciously tried to run as if he still had legs. Was that all there was to it?

George thought of the carnivore again, and of the stalks supporting the organs which he had thought might be eyes. That would do as an experiment. He closed his own eyes and imagined them rising outward, imagined the mobile stalks growing, growing.... He tried to convince himself that he had eyes like that, had always had them—that everyone who was anyone had eyes on stalks.

Surely, something was happening?

George opened his eyes again, and found himself looking straight down at the ground, getting a view so close up that it was blurred, out of focus. Impatiently he tried to look up. All that happened was that his field of vision moved forward a matter of ten or twelve centimeters.

It was at this point that a voice shattered the stillness. It sounded like someone trying to shout through half a meter of lard. 'Urghh! Lluhh! *Eeraghh!*'

George leaped convulsively, executed a neat turn and swept his eyes around a good two hundred and forty degrees of arc. He saw nothing but rocks and lichens. On a closer inspection, it appeared that a small green-and-orange larva or grub of some kind was moving past him. George regarded it with suspicion for a long moment, until the voice broke out again:

'Ellfff! Ellffneee!'

The voice, somewhat higher this time, came from behind. George whirled again, swept his mobile eyes around——

Around an impossible wide circuit. His eyes *were* on stalks, and they were mobile—whereas a moment ago he had been staring at the ground, unable to look up. George's brain clattered into high gear. He had grown stalks for his eyes, all right, but they'd been limp—just extensions of the jellylike mass of his body, without a stiffening cell structure of muscular tissue to move them. Then, when the voice had startled him, he'd got the stiffening and the muscles in a hurry.

That must have been what had happened the previous night. Probably the process would have been completed, but much more slowly, if he hadn't been frightened. A protective mechanism, obviously. As for the voice——

George rotated once more, slowly, looking all around him. There was no question about it: he was alone. The voice, which had seemed to come from someone or something standing just behind him, must in fact have issued from his own body.

The voice started again, at a less frantic volume. It burbled a few times, then said quite clearly in a high tenor, 'Whass happen'? Wheh am I?'

George was floundering in a sea of bewilderment. He was in no condition to adapt quickly to more new circumstances, and when a large, desiccated lump fell from a nearby bush and bounced soundlessly to within a meter of him, he simply stared at it.

He looked at the hard-shelled object, and then at the laden bush from which it had dropped. Slowly, painfully, he worked his way through to a logical conclusion. The dried fruit had fallen without a sound. That was natural, because he had been totally deaf ever since his metamorphosis. But—he had heard a voice!

Ergo, hallucination, or telepathy.

The voice began again. 'He-elp. Oh, dear, I wish someone would answer!'

Vivian Bellis. Gumbs, even if he affected that tenor voice, wouldn't say, 'Oh, dear.' Neither would McCarty.

George's shaken nerves were returning to normal. He thought intently, *I get scared, grow legs. Bellis gets scared, grows a telepathic voice. That's reasonable, I guess—her first and only instinct would be to yell.*

George tried to put himself into a yelling mood. He shut his eyes and imagined himself cooped up in a terrifyingly alien medium, without any control or knowledge of his predicament. He tried to shout: 'Vivian!'

He kept on trying, while the girl's voice continued at intervals. Finally she stopped abruptly in the middle of a sentence. George said, 'Can you hear me?'

'Who's that—what do you want?'

'This is George Meister, Vivian. Can you understand what I'm saying?'

'What——'

George kept at it. His pseudo-voice, he judged, was a little garbled, just as Bellis's had been at first. At least the girl said, 'Oh, George—I mean Mr. Meister! Oh, I've been so frightened. Where are you?'

George explained, apparently not very tactfully, because Bellis shrieked when he was through and then went back to burbling. George sighed, and said, 'Is there anyone else on the premises? Major Gumbs? Miss McCarty?'

A few minutes later two sets of weird sounds began almost simultaneously. When they became coherent, it was no trouble to identify the voices. Gumbs, the big, red-faced professional soldier, shouted, 'Why the hell don't you watch where you're going, Meister? If you hadn't started that rock slide we wouldn't be in this mess!'

Miss McCarty, who had had a seamed white face, a jutting jaw, and eyes the color of mud, said coldly, 'Meister, all of this will be reported. *All* of it.'

It appeared that only Meister and Gumbs had kept the use of their eyes. All four of them had some muscular control, though Gumbs was the only one who had made any serious attempt to interfere with George's locomotion. Miss McCarty, not to George's surprise, had managed to retain a pair of functioning ears.

But Bellis had been blind, deaf and dumb all through the afternoon and night. The only terminal sense organs she had been able to use had been those of the skin—the perceptors of touch, heat and cold, and pain. She had heard nothing, seen nothing, but she had felt every leaf and stalk they had brushed against, the cold impact of every raindrop, and the pain of the toothy monster's bite. George's opinion of her went up several notches when he learned this. She had been terrified, but she hadn't been driven into hysteria or insanity.

It further appeared that nobody was doing any breathing, and nobody was aware of a heartbeat.

George would have liked nothing better than to continue this discussion, but the other three were united in believing that what had happened to them after they got in was of less importance than how they were going to get out.

'We can't get *out*,' said George. 'At least, I don't see any possibility of it in the present state of our knowledge. If we——'

'But we've got to get out!' said Vivian.

'We'll go back to camp,' said McCarty coldly. 'Immediately. And you'll explain to the Loyalty Committee why you didn't turn back as soon as you regained consciousness.'

'That's right,' Gumbs put in self-consciously. 'If you can't do anything, Meister, maybe the other technical fellows can.'

George patiently explained his theory of their probable reception by the guards at the camp. McCarty's keen mind detected a flaw. 'You grew legs, and stalks for your eyes, according to your own testimony. If you weren't lying, you can also grow a mouth. We'll announce ourselves as we approach.'

'That may not be easy,' George told her. 'We couldn't get along with just a mouth, we'd need teeth, tongue, hard and soft palates, lungs or the equivalent, vocal cords, and some kind of substitute for a diaphragm to power the whole business. I'm wondering if it's possible at all, because when Miss Bellis finally succeeded in making herself heard, it was by the method we're using now. She didn't——'

'You talk too much,' said McCarty. 'Major Gumbs, Miss Bellis, you and I will try to form a speaking apparatus. The first to succeed will receive a credit mark on his record. Commence.'

George, being left out of the contest by implication, used his time in trying to restore his hearing. It seemed to him likely that the whatever-it-was *meisterii* had some sort of division-of-labor principle built into it, since Gumbs and he—the first two to fall in—had kept their sight without making any special effort in that direction, while matters like hearing and touch had been left for the latecomers. This was fine in principle, and George approved of it, but he didn't like the idea of Miss McCarty's being the sole custodian of any part of the apparatus.

Even if he were able to persuade the other two to follow his lead—and at the moment this prospect seemed dim—McCarty was certain to be a holdout. And it might easily be vital to all of them, at some time in the near future, to have their hearing hooked into the circuit.

He was distracted at first by muttered comments between Gumbs and Vivian—'Getting anywhere?' 'I don't think so. Are you?'—interspersed between yawps, humming sounds and other irritating noises as they tried unsuccessfully to switch over from mental to vocal communication. Finally McCarty snapped, 'Be quiet. Concentrate on forming the necessary organs—don't bray like jackasses.'

George settled down to his work, using the same technique he had found effective before. With his eyes shut, he imagined that the thing with all the teeth was approaching in darkness—tap, slither; tap; click. He wished valiantly for ears to catch the faint approaching sounds. After a long time he thought he was beginning to succeed—or were those mental sounds, unconsciously emitted by one of the other three? *Click. Slither. Swish. Scrape.*

George opened his eyes, genuinely alarmed. A hundred meters away, facing him across the shallow slope of rocky ground, was a uniformed man just emerging from a stand of black, bamboolike spears. As George raised his eye stalks, the man paused, stared back at him, then shouted and raised his rifle.

George ran. Instantly there was a babble of voices inside him, and the muscles of his 'legs' went into wild spasms. 'Run, dammit!' he said frantically. 'There's a trooper with——'

The rifle went off with a deafening roar, and George felt a sudden hideous pain aft of his spine. Vivian Bellis screamed.

The struggle for possession of their common legs stopped, and they scuttled full speed ahead for the cover of a nearby boulder. The rifle roared again, and George heard rock splinters screeching through the foliage overhead. Then they were plunging down the side of a gully, up the other slope, over a low hummock and into a forest of tall, bare-limbed trees.

George spotted a leaf-filled hollow and headed for it, fighting somebody else's desire to keep on running in a straight line. They plopped into the hollow and stayed there while three running men went past them, and for an hour afterward.

Vivian was moaning steadily. Raising his eye stalks cautiously, George was able to see that several jagged splinters of stone had penetrated the monster's gelatinous flesh near the far rim. . . . They had been very lucky. The shot had apparently been a near miss—accountable only on the grounds that the trooper had been shooting downhill at a moving target—and had shattered the boulder behind them.

Looking more closely, George observed something which excited his professional interest. The whole surface of the monster appeared to be in constant slow ferment: tiny pits opening and closing as if the flesh were boiling . . . except that here the bubbles of air were not forcing their way outward, but were being engulfed at the surface and pressed down into the interior.

He could also see, deep under the mottled surface of the huge lens-shaped body, four vague clots of darkness which must be the living brains of Gumbs, Bellis, McCarty—and Meister.

Yes, there was one which was radially opposite his own eye stalks. It was an odd thing, George reflected, to be looking at your own brain. No doubt you could get used to it in time.

The four dark spots were arranged close together in an almost perfect square at the center of the lens. The spinal cords, barely visible, crossed between them and rayed outward from the center.

Pattern, George thought. The thing was designed to make use of more than one nervous system. It arranged them in an orderly fashion, with the brains inward for greater protection —and perhaps for another reason. Perhaps there was even a provision for conscious cooperation among the passengers: a matrix that somehow promoted the growth of communication cells between separate brains.... If that were so, it would account for their ready success with telepathy. George wished most acutely that he could get inside and find out.

Vivian's pain was diminishing. Hers was the brain opposite George's, and she had taken most of the effect of the rock splinters. But the fragments were sinking now, slowly, through the gelid substance of the monster's tissues. Watching carefully, George could see them move. When they got to the bottom, they would be excreted, no doubt—just as the indigestible parts of their clothing and equipment had been.

George wondered idly which of the remaining two brains was McCarty's and which Gumbs's. The answer was easy to find. To George's left, as he looked back toward the center of the mound, was a pair of blue eyes set flush with the surface. They had lids apparently grown from the monster's substance, but thickened and opaque.

To his right, George could make out two tiny openings, extending a few centimeters into the body, which could only be Miss McCarty's ears. George had an impulse to see if he could devise a method of dropping dirt into them.

Anyhow, the question of returning to camp had been settled, at least for the moment. McCarty said nothing more about growing a set of speech organs, although George was sure she herself was determined to keep on trying.

He didn't think she would succeed. Whatever the mechanism was by which these changes in bodily structure were accomplished, it seemed probable that amateurs like themselves could succeed only under the pressure of considerable emotional strain, and then only with comparatively simple tasks which involved one new structure at a time. And as he had already told McCarty, the speech organs in man were extraordinarily diverse and complicated.

It occurred to George that the thing just might be done by creating a thin membrane to serve as a diaphragm, and an air chamber behind it, with a set of muscles to produce the neces-

23

sary vibrations and modulate them. He kept the notion to himself.

He didn't want to go back. George was a rare bird: a scientist who was actually fitted for his work and loved it for its own sake. And at the moment he was sitting squarely in the middle of the most powerful research tool that had ever existed in his field: a protean organism, with the observer inside it, able to order its structure and watch the results; able to devise theories of function and test them on the tissues of what was effectively his own body—able to construct new organs, new adaptations to environment!

George saw himself at the point of an enormous cone of new knowledge; and some of the possibilities he glimpsed humbled and awed him.

He *couldn't* go back, even if it were possible to do it without getting killed. If only he had fallen into the damned thing alone—— No, then the others would have pulled him out and killed the monster.

There were, he felt, too many problems demanding solutions all at once. It was hard to concentrate; his mind kept slipping maddeningly out of focus.

Vivian, whose pain had stopped some time ago, began to wail again. Gumbs snapped at her. McCarty cursed both of them. George himself felt that he had had very nearly all he could take—cooped up with three idiots who had no more sense than to——

'Wait a minute,' he said. 'Do you all feel the same way? Irritable? Jumpy? As if you'd been working for sixty hours straight and were too tired to sleep?'

'Stop talking like a video ad,' Vivian said angrily. 'Haven't we got enough trouble without——'

'We're hungry,' George interrupted. 'We didn't realise it, because we haven't got the organs that usually signal hunger. But the last thing this body ate was *us*, and that was at least twenty hours ago. We've got to find something to ingest.'

'Good Lord, you're right,' said Gumbs. 'But if this thing only eats people—I mean to say——'

'It never met any people until we landed,' George said curtly. 'Any protein should do, but the only way we can find

24

out is to try. The sooner we start, the better.'

He started off in what he hoped was the direction they had been following all along—directly away from camp. At least, he thought, if they put enough distance behind them, they might get thoroughly lost.

II

They moved out of the trees and down the long slope of a valley, over a wiry carpet of dead grasses, until they reached a watercourse in which a thin trickle was still flowing. Far down the bank, partly screened by clumps of skeletal shrubbery, George saw a group of animals that looked vaguely like miniature pigs. He told the others about it, and started cautiously in that direction.

'Which way is the wind blowing, Vivian?' he asked. 'Can you feel it?'

She said, 'No. I could before, when we were going downhill, but now I think we're facing into it.'

'Good,' said George. 'We may be able to sneak up on them.'

'But—we're not going to eat *animals*, are we?'

'Yes, how about it, Meister?' Gumbs put in. 'I don't say I'm a squeamish fellow, but after all——'

George, who felt a little squeamish himself—like all the others, he had been brought up on a diet of yeasts and synthetic protein—said testily, 'What else can we do? You've got eyes—you can see it's autumn here. Autumn after a hot summer, at that. Trees bare, streams dried up. We eat meat, or go without—unless you'd rather hunt for insects?'

Gumbs, shocked to the core, muttered for a while and then gave up.

Seen at closer range, the animals looked less porcine and even less appetising than before. They had lean, segmented, pinkish-gray bodies, four short legs, flaring ears and blunt scimitarlike snouts with which they were rooting in the ground, occasionally turning up something which they gulped, ears flapping.

George counted thirty of them, grouped fairly closely in a little space of clear ground between the bushes and the river. They moved slowly, but their short legs looked powerful; he

25

guessed that they could run when they had to.

He inched forward, keeping his eye stalks low, stopping instantly whenever one of the beasts looked up. Moving with increasing caution, he had got to within ten meters of the nearest when McCarty said abruptly:

'Meister, has it occurred to you to wonder just *how* we are going to eat these animals?'

'Don't be foolish,' he said irritably. 'We'll——' He stopped.

Wait a minute—did the thing's normal method of assimilation stop as soon as it got a tenant? Were they supposed to grow fangs and a gullet and all the rest of the apparatus? Impossible; they'd starve to death first. But on the other hand —*damn* this fuzzy-headed feeling—wouldn't it have to stop, to prevent the tenant from being digested with the first meal?

'Well?' McCarty demanded.

That was wrong, George knew, but he couldn't say why; and it was a distinctly unpleasant thought. Or—even worse— suppose the meal became the tenant, and the tenant the meal?

The nearest animal's head went up, and four tiny red eyes stared at George. The floppy ears snapped to attention.

It was no time for speculation. 'He's seen us!' George shouted mentally. '*Run!*'

The scene exploded into motion. One instant they were lying still in the prickly dry grass; the next they were skimming at express-train speed across the ground, with the herd galloping away straight ahead of them. The hams of the nearest beast loomed up closer and closer, bounding furiously; then they had run it down and vaulted over it.

Casting an eye backward, George saw that it was lying motionless in the grass—unconscious or dead.

They ran down another one. *The anaesthetic*, George thought lucidly. *One touch does it.* And another, and another. *Of course we can digest them,* he thought with relief. *It has to be selective to begin with, or it couldn't have separated out our nervous tissue.*

Four down. Six down. Three more together as the herd bunched between the last arm of the thicket and the steep river bank; then two that tried to double back; then four stragglers, one after the other.

The rest of the herd disappeared into the tall grass up the slope; but fifteen bodies were strewn behind them.

Taking no chances, George went back to the beginning of the line and edged the monster's body under the first carcass.

'Crouch down, Gumbs,' he said. 'We have to slide under it ... that's far enough. Leave the head hanging over.'

'What for?' said the soldier.

'You don't want his brain in here with us, do you? We don't know how many this thing is equipped to take. It might even like this one better than one of ours. But I can't see it bothering to keep the rest of the nervous system, if we make sure not to eat the head——'

'Oh!' said Vivian faintly.

'I beg your pardon, Miss Bellis,' George said contritely. 'It shouldn't be too unpleasant, though, if we don't let it bother us. It isn't as if we had taste buds, or——'

'It's all right,' she said. 'Just please let's not talk about it.'

'I should think not,' Gumbs put in. 'A little more tact, don't you think, Meister?'

Accepting this reproof, George turned his attention to the corpse that lay on the monster's glabrous surface, between his section and Gumbs's. It was sinking, just visibly, into the flesh. A cloud of opacity was spreading around it.

When it was almost gone, and the neck had been severed, they moved on to the next. This time, at George's suggestion, they took aboard two at once. Gradually their irritable mood faded; they began to feel at ease and cheerful, and George found it possible to think consecutively without having vital points slip out of his reach.

They were in their eighth and ninth courses, and George was happily engaged in an intricate chain of speculation as to the monster's circulatory system, when Miss McCarty broke a long silence to announce:

'I have now perfected a method by which we can return to camp safely. We will begin at once.'

Startled and dismayed, George turned his eyes toward McCarty's quadrant of the monster. Protruding from the rim was a stringy, jointed something that looked like—yes, it

27

was!—a grotesque but recognisable arm and hand. As he watched, the lumpy fingers fumbled with a blade of grass, tugged, uprooted it.

'Major Gumbs!' said McCarty. 'It will be your task to locate the following articles, as quickly as possible. One. A surface suitable for writing. I suggest a large leaf, light in color, dry but not brittle. Or a tree from which a large section of bark can be easily peeled. Two. A pigment. No doubt you will be able to discover berries yielding suitable juice. If not, mud will do. Three. A twig or reed for use as a pen. When you have directed me to all these essential items, I will employ them to write a message outlining our predicament. You will read the result and point out any errors, which I will then correct. When the message is completed, we will return with it to the camp, approaching at night, and deposit it in a conspicuous place. We will retire until daybreak, and when the message has been read we will approach again. Begin, Major.'

'Well, yes,' said Gumbs, 'that ought to work, except—I suppose you've worked out some system for holding the pen, Miss McCarty?'

'Fool,' she replied, 'I have made a hand, of course.'

'Well, in that case, by all means. Let's see, I believe we might try this thicket first——' Their common body gave a lurch in that direction.

George held back. 'Wait a minute,' he said desperately. 'Let's at least have the common sense to finish this meal before we go. There's no telling when we'll get another.'

McCarty demanded, 'How large are these creatures, Major?'

'Oh—about sixty centimeters long, I should say.'

'And we have consumed nine of them, is that correct?'

'Nearer eight,' George said. 'These two are only half gone.'

'In other words,' McCarty said, 'we have had two apiece. That should be ample. Don't you agree, Major?'

George said earnestly, 'You're wrong, Miss McCarty. You're thinking in terms of human food requirements, whereas this organism has a different metabolic rate and at least three times the mass of four human beings. Look at it this way—the four of us together had a mass of about three hundred kilos

28

and yet twenty hours after this thing absorbed us, it was hungry again. Well, these animals wouldn't weigh much more than twenty kilos apiece at one G—and according to your scheme we've got to hold out until sometime after daybreak tomorrow.'

'Something in that,' Gumbs said. 'Yes, on the whole, Miss McCarty, I think we had better forage while we can. It won't take us more than half and hour longer, at this rate.'

'Very well. Be as quick as you can.'

They moved on to the next pair of victims. George's brain was working furiously. It was no good arguing with McCarty, and Gumbs was not much better, but he had to try. If he could only convince Gumbs, then Bellis would fall in with the majority—maybe. It was the only hope he had.

'Gumbs,' he said, 'have you given any thought to what's going to happen to us when we get back?'

'Not quite my line, you know. Leave that to the technical fellows like yourself.'

'No, that isn't what I mean. Suppose you were the C.O. of this team, and four people had fallen into this organism instead of us——'

'What, what? I don't follow.'

George patiently repeated it.

'Yes, I see what you mean. And so——'

'What orders would you give?'

Gumbs thought a moment. 'Turn the thing over to the bio section, I suppose. What else?'

'You don't think you might order it destroyed as a possible menace?'

'Good Lord, I suppose I might. No, but you see, we'll be careful what we say in the note. We'll point out that we're a valuable specimen, and so on. Handle with care.'

'All right,' George said, 'but suppose that works, then what? Since it's out of your line, I'll tell you, Nine chances out of ten, bio section will classify us as a possible enemy weapon. That means, first of all, that we'll go through a full-dress interrogation—and I don't have to tell you what that can be like.'

'Major Gumbs,' said McCarty stridently, 'Meister will be

executed for disloyalty at the first opportunity. You are forbidden to talk to him, under the same penalty.'

'But she can't stop you from listening to me,' George said tensely. 'In the second place, Gumbs, they'll take samples. Without anaesthesia. And finally, they'll either destroy us just the same, or they'll send us back to the nearest strong point for more study. We will then be Federation property, Gumbs, in a top-secret category, and since nobody in Intelligence will ever dare to take the responsibility of clearing us, we'll *stay* there.

'Gumbs, this *is* a valuable specimen, but it will never do anybody any good if we go back to camp. Whatever we discover about it, even if it's knowledge that could save billions of lives, that will be top-secret too, and it'll never get past the walls of Intelligence. . . . If you're still hoping that they can get you out of this, you're wrong. This isn't like limb grafts, *your whole body* has been destroyed, Gumbs, everything but your nervous system and your eyes. The only new body we'll get is the one we make ourselves. We've got to stay here and—and work this out ourselves.'

'Major Gumbs,' said McCarty, 'I think we have wasted quite enough time. Begin your search for the materials I need.'

For a moment Gumbs was silent, and their collective body did not move.

Then he said: 'Yes, that was a leaf, a twig and a bunch of berries, wasn't it? Or mud. Miss McCarty, unofficially of course, there's one point I'd like your opinion on. Before we begin. That is to say, I daresay they'll be able to patch together some sort of bodies for us, don't you think? I mean, one technical fellow says one thing, another says the opposite. Do you see what I'm driving at?'

George had been watching McCarty's new limb uneasily. It was flexing rhythmically and, he was almost certain, growing minutely larger. The fingers groped occasionally in the dry grass, plucking first a single blade, then two together, finally a whole tuft. Now she said: 'I have no opinion, Major. The question is irrelevant. Out duty is to return to camp. That is all we need to know.'

'Oh, I quite agree with you there,' said Gumbs. 'And besides, there really isn't any alternative, is there?'

George, staring down at one of the fingerlike projections visible below the rim of the monster, was passionately willing it to turn into an arm. He had, he suspected, started much too late.

'The alternative,' he said, 'is simply to keep on going as we are. Even if the Federation holds this planet for a century, there'll be places on it that will never be explored. We'll be safe.'

'I mean to say,' added Gumbs as if he had only paused for thought, 'a fellow can't very well cut himself off from civilisation, can he?'

Again George felt a movement toward the thicket; again he resisted it. Then he found himself overpowered, as another set of muscles joined themselves to Gumbs's. Quivering, crabwise, the something *meisterii* moved half a meter. Then it stopped, straining.

And for the second time that day, George was forced to revise his opinion of Vivian Bellis.

'I believe you, Mr. Meister—George,' she said. 'I don't want to go back. Tell me what you want me to do.'

'You're doing beautifully now,' George said after a speechless instant. 'Except if you can grow an arm, I imagine that will be useful.'

The struggle went on.

'Now we know where we are,' said McCarty to Gumbs.

'Yes. Quite right.'

'Major Gumbs,' she said crisply, 'you are opposite me, I believe?'

'Am I?' said Gumbs doubtfully.

'Never mind. I believe you are. Now: is Meister to your right or left?'

'Left. I know that, anyhow. Can see his eye stalks out of the corner of my eye.'

'Very well.' McCarty's arm rose, with a sharp-pointed fragment of rock clutched in the blobby fingers.

Horrified, George watched it bend backward across the curve of the monster's body. The long, knife-sharp point probed tentatively at the surface three centimeters short of the

31

area over his brain. Then the fist made an abrupt up-and-down movement, and a fierce stab of pain shot through him.

'Not quite long enough, I think,' McCarty said. She flexed the arm, then brought it back to almost the same spot and stabbed again.

'No,' she said thoughtfully. 'It will take a little longer,' then, 'Major Gumbs, after my next attempt you will tell me if you notice any reaction in Meister's eye stalks.'

The pain was still throbbing along George's nerves. With one half-blinded eye he watched the embryonic arm that was growing, too slowly, under the rim; with the other, fascinated, he watched McCarty's arm lengthen slowly toward him.

It was growing visibly, he suddenly realised—but it wasn't getting any nearer. In fact, incredibly enough, it seemed to be losing ground.

The monster's flesh was flowing away under it, expanding in both directions.

McCarty stabbed again, with vicious strength. This time the pain was less acute.

'Major?' she said. 'Any result?'

'No,' said Gumbs, 'no, I think not. We seem to be moving forward a bit, though, Miss McCarty.'

'A ridiculous error,' she replied. 'We are being forced *back*. Pay attention, Major.'

'No, really,' he protested. 'That is to say, we're moving toward the thicket. Forward to me, backward to you.'

'Major Gumbs, *I* am moving forward, *you* are moving back.'

They were both right, George discovered: the monster's body was no longer circular, it was extending itself along the Gumbs–McCarty axis. A suggestion of concavity was becoming visible in the center. Below the surface, too, there was motion.

The four brains now formed an oblong, not a square.

The positions of the spinal cords had shifted. His own and Vivian's seemed to be about where they were, but Gumbs's now passed under McCarty's brain, and vice versa.

Having increased its mass by some two hundred kilos, the something *meisterii* was fissioning into two individuals—and

32

tidily separating its tenants, two to each. Gumbs and Meister in one, McCarty and Bellis in the other.

The next time it happened, he realised, each product of the fission would be reduced to one brain—and the time after that, one of the new individuals out of each pair would be a monster in the primary or untenanted state, quiescent, camouflaged, waiting to be stumbled over.

But that meant that, like the common amoeba, this fascinating organism was immortal. It never died, barring accidents; it simply grew and divided.

Not the tenants, though, unfortunately—their tissues would wear out and die.

Or would they? Human nervous tissue didn't proliferate as George's and Miss McCarty's had done; neither did *any* human tissue build new cells fast enough to account for George's eye stalks or Miss McCarty's arm.

There was no question about it: none of that new tissue could possibly be human; it was all counterfeit, produced by the monster from its own substance according to the structural blueprints in the nearest genuine cells. And it was a perfect counterfeit: the new tissues knit with the old, axones coupled with dendrites, muscles contracted or expanded on command. The imitation *worked*.

And therefore, when nerve cells wore out, they could be replaced. Eventually the last human cell would go, the human tenant would have become totally monster—but 'a difference that makes no difference is no difference.' Effectively, the tenant would still be human—and he would be immortal.

Barring accidents.

Or murder.

Miss McCarty was saying, 'Major Gumbs, you are being ridiculous. The explanation is quite obvious. Unless you are deliberately deceiving me, for what reason I cannot imagine, then our efforts to move in opposing directions must be pulling this creature apart.'

McCarty was evidently confused by her geometry. Let her stay that way—it would keep her off balance until the fission was complete. No, that was no good. George himself was out of her reach already, and getting farther away—but how about

Bellis? Her brain and McCarty's were, if anything, closer together. . . .

What to do? If he warned the girl, that would only draw McCarty's attention to her sooner. Unless he could misdirect her at the same time——

There wasn't much time left, he realised abruptly. If he was right in thinking that some physical linkage between the brains had occurred to make communication possible, those cells couldn't hold out much longer; the gap between the two pairs of brains was widening steadily.

'Vivian!' he said.

'Yes, George?'

Relieved, he said rapidly. 'Listen, we're not pulling this body apart, it's splitting. That's the way it reproduces. You and I will be in one half, Gumbs and McCarty in the other. If they don't give us any trouble, we can all go where we please——'

'Oh, I'm so glad!'

What a warm voice she had. . . . 'Yes,' said George nervously, 'but we may have to fight them; it's up to them. So *grow an arm*, Vivian.'

'I'll try,' she said doubtfully. 'I don't know——'

McCarty's voice cut across hers. 'Ah. Major Gumbs, since you have eyes, it will be your task to see to it that those two do not escape. Meanwhile, I suggest that you, also, grow an arm.'

'Doing my best,' said Gumbs.

Puzzled, George glanced downward, past his own half-formed arm: there, almost out of sight, was a fleshy bulge under Gumbs's section of the rim! The major had been working on it in secret, keeping it hidden . . . and it was already better developed than George's.

'Oh-oh,' said Gumbs abruptly. 'Look here, Miss McCarty, Meister's been leading you up the garden path. Look here, I mean, you and I aren't going to be in the same half. How could we be? We're on *opposite sides* of the blasted thing. It's going to be you and Miss Bellis, me and Meister.'

The monster was developing a definite waistline. The spinal cords had rotated, now, so that there was clear space between them in the center.

'Yes,' said McCarty faintly. '*Thank* you, Major Gumbs.'

'George!' came Vivian's frightened voice, distant and weak. 'What shall I do?'

'Grow an arm!' he shouted.

There was no reply.

III

Frozen, George watched McCarty's arm, the rock-fragment still clutched at the end of it, rise into view and swing leftward at full stretch over the bubbling surface of the monster. He had time to see it bob up and viciously down again; time to think, *Still short, thank God—that's McCarty's right arm, it's farther from Vivian's brain than it was from mine;* time, finally, to realise that he could not possibly help her before McCarty lengthened the arm a few centimeters more than were necessary. The fission was not more than half complete; and he could no more move to where he wanted to be than a Siamese twin could walk around his brother.

Then his time was up. A flicker of motion warned him, and he looked back to see a lumpy, distorted pseudo-hand clutching for his eye stalks.

Instinctively he brought his own hand up, grasped the other's wrist and hung on desperately. It was half again the size of his, and so strongly muscled that although his leverage was better, he couldn't force it back or hold it away; he could only keep the system oscillating up and down, adding his strength to Gumbs's so that the mark was overshot.

Gumbs began to vary the force and rhythm of his movements, trying to catch him off guard. A thick finger brushed the base of one eye stalk.

'Sorry about this, Meister,' said Gumbs's voice. 'No hard feelings in it, on my side. Between us (oof) I don't fancy that McCarty woman much—but (ugh! almost had you that time) beggars can't be choosers. Ah. Way I see it, I've got to look after myself; mean to say (ugh) if I don't, who will? See what I mean?'

George did not reply. Astonishingly enough, he was no longer afraid, either for himself or for Vivian; he was simply overpoweringly, ecstatically, monomaniacally angry. Power

35

from somewhere was surging into his arm; fiercely concentrating, he thought *Bigger! Stronger! Longer! More arm!*

The arm grew. Visibly it added substance to itself, it lengthened, thickened, bulged with muscle. So did Gumbs's.

He began another arm. So did Gumbs.

All around him the surface of the monster was bubbling violently. And, George realised finally, the lenticular bulk of it was perceptibly shrinking. Its curious breathing system was inadequate; the thing was cannibalising itself, destroying its own tissues to make up the difference.

How small could it get and still support two human tenants?

And which brain would it dispense with first?

He had no leisure to think about it. Scrabbling in the grass with his second hand, Gumbs had failed to find anything that would serve as a weapon; now, with a sudden lurch, he swung their entire body around.

The fission was complete.

That thought reminded George of Vivian and McCarty. He risked a split second's glance behind him, saw nothing but a featureless ovoid mound, and looked back in time to see Gumbs's half-grown right fist pluck a long, sharp-pointed dead branch out of the grass. In the next instant the thing came whipping at his eyes.

The lip of the river bank was a meter away to the left. George made it in one abrupt surge. They slipped, tottered, hesitated, hands clutching wildly—and toppled, end over end, hurtling in a cloud of dust and pebbles down the breakneck slope to a meaty smash at the bottom.

The universe made one more giant turn around them and came to rest. Half blinded, George groped for the hold he had lost, found the wrist and seized it.

'Oh, Lord,' said Gumbs's voice, 'that's done me. I'm hurt, Meister. Go on, man, finish it, will you? Don't waste time.'

George stared at him suspiciously, without relaxing his grip. 'What's the matter with you?'

'I tell you I'm done,' said Gumbs pettishly. 'Paralysed. I can't move.'

They had fallen, George saw, onto a small boulder, one of

many with which the river bed was strewn. This one was roughly conical; they were draped over it, and the blunt point was directly under Gumbs's spinal cord, a few centimeters from the brain.

'Gumbs,' he said, 'that may not be as bad as you think. If I can show you it isn't, will you give up and put yourself under my orders?'

'How do you mean? My spine's crushed.'

'Never mind that now. Will you or won't you?'

'Why, yes,' said Gumbs. 'That's very decent of you, Meister, matter of fact. You have my word, for what it's worth.'

'All right,' said George. Straining hard, he managed to get their body down off the boulder. Then he stared up at the slope down which they had tumbled. Too steep; he'd have to find an easier way back. He turned and started off to eastward, paralleling the thin stream that still flowed in the center of the watercourse.

'What's up now?' Gumbs asked after a moment.

'We've got to find a way up to the top,' George said impatiently. 'I may still be able to help Vivian.'

'Ah, yes. Afraid I was thinking about myself, Meister. If you don't mind telling me——'

She couldn't still be alive, George was thinking despondently, but if there were any small chance—— 'You'll be all right,' he said. 'If you were still in your old body that would be a fatal injury, or permanently disabling, anyhow, but not in this thing. You can repair yourself as easily as you can grow a new limb.'

'Good Lord,' said Gumbs. 'Stupid of me not to think of that. But look here, Meister, does that mean we were simply wasting our time trying to kill one another? I mean to say——'

'No. If you'd crushed my brain, I think the organism would have digested it, and that would be the end of me. But short of anything that drastic, I believe we're immortal.'

'Immortal,' said Gumbs. 'Good Lord.... That does rather put another face on it, doesn't it?'

The bank was becoming a little lower, and at one point,

where the raw earth was thickly seeded with boulders, there was a talus slope that looked as if it could be climbed. George started up it.

'Meister,' said Gumbs after a moment.

'What do you want?'

'You're right, you know—I'm getting some feeling back already.... Look here, Meister, is there anything this beast *can't* do? I mean, for instance, do you suppose we could put ourselves back together the way we were, with all the—appendages, and so on?'

'It's possible,' George said curtly. It was a thought that had been in the back of his mind, but he didn't feel like discussing it with Gumbs just now.

They were halfway up the slope.

'Well, in that case——' said Gumbs meditatively. 'The thing has *military* possibilities, you know. Man who brought a thing like that direct to the War Department could write his own ticket, more or less.'

'After we split up,' George said, 'you can do whatever you please.'

'But, dammit,' said Gumbs in an irritated tone, 'that won't do.'

'Why not?'

'Because,' said Gumbs, 'they might find you.' His hands reached up abruptly, grasped a small boulder, and before George could stop him, pried it sidewise out of its socket in the earth.

The larger boulder above it trembled, dipped and leaned ponderously outward. George, directly underneath, found that he could move neither forward nor back.

'Sorry again,' he heard Gumbs saying, with what sounded like genuine regret. 'But you know the Loyalty Committee. I simply can't take the chance.'

The boulder seemed to take forever to fall. George tried twice more, with all his strength, to move out of its path. Then, instinctively, he put his arms straight under it.

At the last possible instant he moved them to the left, away from the center of the toppling gray mass.

38

It struck.

George felt his arms breaking like twigs, and saw a loom-ing grayness that blotted out the sky; he felt a sledge-hammer impact that made the earth shudder beneath him.

He heard a splattering sound.

And he was still alive. That astonishing fact kept him fully occupied for a long time after the boulder had clattered its way down the slope into silence. Then, finally, he looked down to his right.

The resistance of his stiffened arms, even while they broke, had been barely enough to lever the falling body over, a dis-tance of some thirty centimeters.... The right half of the monster was a flattened shattered ruin. He could see a few flecks of pasty gray matter, melting now into green-brown translucence as the mass flowed slowly together again.

In twenty minutes the last remains of a superfluous spinal cord had been reabsorbed, the monster had collected itself back into its normal lens shape, and George's pain was dimin-ishing. In five minutes more his mended arms were strong enough to use. They were also more convincingly shaped and colored than before—the tendons, the fingernails, even the wrinkles of the skin were in good order. In ordinary circum-stances this discovery would have left George happily be-mused for hours; now, in his impatience, he barely noticed it. He climbed to the top of the bank.

Thirty meters away a humped green-brown body like his own lay motionless in the dry grass.

It contained, of course, only one brain. Whose?

McCarty's, almost certainly; Vivian hadn't had a chance. But then how did it happen that there was no visible trace of McCarty's arm?

Unnerved, George walked around the creature for a closer inspection.

On the far side he encountered two dark-brown eyes, with an oddly unfinished appearance. They focused on him after an instant, and the whole body quivered slightly, moving toward him.

Vivian's eyes had been brown; George remembered them distinctly. Brown eyes with heavy dark lashes in a tapering slender face.... But did that prove anything? What color had McCarty's eyes been? He couldn't remember for certain.

There was only one way to find out. George moved closer, hoping fervently that the something *meisterii* was at least advanced enough to conjugate, instead of trying to devour members of its own species....

The two bodies touched, clung and began to flow together. Watching, George saw the fissioning process reverse itself: from paired lenses the alien flesh melted into a slipper shape, to an ovoid, to lens shape again. His brain and the other drifted closer together, the spinal cords crossing at right angles.

And it was only then that he noticed an oddity about the other brain: it seemed to be lighter and larger than his, the outline a trifle sharper.

'Vivian?' he said doubtfully. 'Is that you?'

No answer. He tried again; and again.

Finally:

'George! Oh dear—I want to cry, but I can't seem to do it.'

'No lachrymal glands,' George said automatically. 'Uh, Vivian?'

'Yes, George.' That warm voice again....

'What happened to Miss McCarty? How did you—I mean, what happened?'

'I don't know. She's gone, isn't she? I haven't heard her for a long time.'

'Yes,' said George, 'she's gone. You mean you don't *know*? Tell me what you did.'

'Well, I wanted to make an arm, because you told me to, but I didn't think I had time enough. So I made a skull instead. And those things to cover my spine——'

'Vertebrae.' *Now why*, he thought dazedly, *didn't I think of that*? 'And then?' he said.

'I think I'm crying now,' she said. 'Yes, I am. It's such a relief. And then, after that, nothing. She was still hurting me, and I just lay here and thought how wonderful it would be if she weren't in here with me. And then, after a while, she wasn't. Then I grew eyes to look for you.'

40

The explanation, it seemed to George, was more perplexing than the enigma. Staring around in a vague search for enlightenment, he caught sight of something that had escaped his notice before. Two meters to his left, just visible in the grass, was a damp-looking grayish lump, with a suggestion of a stringy extension trailing off from it. . . .

There must, he decided suddenly, be some mechanism in the something *meisterii* for disposing of tenants who failed to adapt themselves—brains that went into catatonia, or hysteria, or suicidal frenzy. An eviction clause.

Somehow, Vivian had managed to stimulate that mechanism—to convince the organism that McCarty's brain was not only superfluous but dangerous—'poisonous' was the word.

Miss McCarty—it was the final ignominy—had not been digested, but excreted.

By sunset, twelve hours later, they had made a good deal of progress. They had reached an understanding very agreeable to them both; they had hunted down another herd of the pseudo-pigs for their noon meal; and, for divergent reasons—on George's side because the monster's normal metabolism was grossly inefficient when it had to move quickly, and on Vivian's because she refused to believe that any man could be attracted to her in her present condition—they had begun a serious attempt to reshape themselves.

The first trials were extraordinarily difficult, the rest surprisingly easy. Again and again they had to let themselves collapse back into amoeboid masses, victims of some omitted or malfunctioning organ; but each failure smoothed the road; eventually they were able to stand breathless but breathing, swaying but erect, face to face—two protean giants in the fortunate dimness, two sketches of self-created Man.

They had also put thirty kilometers between themselves and the Federation camp. Standing on the crest of a rise and looking southward across the shallow valley, George could see a faint funereal glow: the mining machines, chewing out metals to feed the fabricators that would spawn a billion ships.

'We'll never go back, will we?' said Vivian.

'No,' said George soberly. 'They'll come to us, in time. We

41

have lots of time. We're the future.'

And one thing more, a small thing, but important to George; it marked his sense of accomplishment, of one phase ended and a new one begun. He had finally completed the name of his discovery—not, as it turned out, anything *meisterii* at all. *Spes hominis*:

Man's hope.

AN EYE FOR A WHAT?

I

On his way across the wheel one morning, Dr. Walter Alvarez detoured down to C level promenade. A few men were standing, as usual, at the window looking out at the enormous blue-green planet below. They were dressed alike in sheen-gray coveralls, a garment with detachable gauntlets and hood designed to make it convertible into a spacesuit. It was uncomfortable, but regulation: according to the books, a Survey and Propaganda Satellite might find itself under attack at any moment.

Nothing so interesting had happened to SAPS 3107A, orbiting the seventh planet of a G-type star in Ophiuchus. They had been here for two years and a half, and most of them had not even touched ground yet.

There it was, drifting by out there, blue-green, fat and juicy —an oxygen planet, two-thirds land, mild climate, soil fairly bursting with minerals and organics.

Alvarez felt his mouth watering when he looked at it. He had 'wheel fever'; they all did. He wanted to get *down* there, to natural gravity and natural ailments.

The last month or so, there had been a feeling in the satellite that a break-through was coming. Always coming: it never arrived.

A plump orthotypist named Lola went by, and a couple of the men turned with automatic whistles. 'Listen,' said Olaf Marx conspiratorially, with a hand on Alvarez's arm, 'that reminds me, did you hear what happened at the big banquet yesterday?'

'No,' said Alvarez, irritably withdrawing his arm. 'I didn't go. Can't stand banquets. Why?'

'Well, the way I got it, the Commandant's wife was sitting right across from George——'

43

Alvarez's interest sharpened. 'You mean the gorgon? What did he do?'

'I'm *telling* you. See, it looked like he was watching her all through dinner. Then up comes the dessert—lemon meringue. So old George——'

The shift bell rang. Alvarez started nervously and looked at his thumbwatch. The other men were drifting away. So was Olaf, laughing like a fool. 'You'll die when you hear,' he called back. 'Boy, do I wish I'd been there myself! So long, Walt.'

Alvarez reluctantly went the other way. In B corridor, somebody called after him, 'Hey, Walt? Hear about the banquet?'

He shook his head. The other man, a baker named Pedro, grinned and waved, disappearing up the curve of the corridor. Alvarez opened the door of Xenology Section and went in.

During his absence, somebody had put a new chart on the wall. It was ten feet high and there were little rectangles all over it, each connected by lines to other rectangles. When he first saw it, Alvarez thought it was a new table of organisation for the Satellite Service, and he winced: but on closer inspection, the chart was *too* complex, and besides, it had a peculiar disorganised appearance. Boxes had been white-rubbed out and other boxes drawn on top of them. Some parts were crowded illegibly together and others were spacious. The whole thing looked desperately confused; and so did Elvis Womrath, who was on a wheeled ladder erasing the entire top righthand corner. 'N panga,' he said irritably. 'That right?'

'Yes,' a voice piped unexpectedly. Alvarez looked around, saw nobody. The voice went on, 'But he is R panga to his cousins and all their N pangas or bigger, except when——'

Alvarez leaned over and peered around the desk. There on the carpet was the owner of the voice, a pinkish-white spheroid with various appendages sprouting in all directions, like a floating mine: 'George' the gorgon. 'Oh, it's you,' said Alvarez, producing his echo sounder and humidometer. 'What's all this nonsense I hear——' He began to prod the gorgon with the test equipment, making his regular morning examination. It was the only bright moment of his day; the infirmary could wait.

'All right,' Womrath interrupted, scrubbing furiously. 'R panga to cousins—wait a minute, now.' He turned with a scowl. 'Alvarez, I'll be through in a minute. N panga or bigger, except when ...' He sketched in half a dozen boxes, labeled them and began to draw connecting lines. 'Now is *that* right?' he asked George.

'Yes, only now it is wrong panga to *mother*'s cousins. Draw again, from father's cousins' N pangas, to mother's cousins O pangas or bigger ... Yes, and now from father's uncles' R pangas, to mother's uncles' pangas *cousins*——'

Womrath's hand faltered. He stared at the chart; he had drawn such a tangle of lines, he couldn't tell what box connected with which. 'Oh, God,' he said hopelessly. He climbed down off the ladder and slapped the stylus into Alvarez's palm. '*You* go nuts.' He thumbed the intercom on the desk and said, 'Chief, I'm going off now. *Way* off.'

'*Did you get that chart straightened out?*' the intercom demanded.

'No, but——'

'*You're on extra duty as of now. Take a pill. Is Alvarez here?*'

'Yes,' said Womrath resignedly.

'*Both of you come in, then. Leave George outside.*'

'Hello, Doctor,' the spheroid piped. 'Are you panga to me?'

'Don't let's go into *that*,' said Womrath, twitching, and took Alvarez by the sleeve. They found the chief of the Xenology Section, Edward H. Dominick, huddled bald and bearlike behind his desk. The cigar in his hand looked chewed. 'Womrath,' he said, 'when can you give me that chart?'

'I don't know. Never, maybe.' When Dominick scowled at him irritably, he shrugged and lit a sullen cigarette.

Dominick swiveled his gaze to Alvarez. 'Have you,' he asked, 'heard about what happened at the banquet in George's honor yesterday?'

'No, I have not,' said Alvarez. 'Will you be so kind as to tell me, or else shut up about it?'

Dominick rubbed his shaven skull, absorbing the insult. 'It was during the dessert,' he said. 'George was sitting opposite Mrs. Carver, in that little jump seat. Just as she got her fork into the pie—it was lemon meringue—George rolled up over the table and grabbed the plate away. Mrs. Carver screamed, pulled back—thought she was being attacked, I suppose—and the chair went out from under her. It—was—a—mess.'

Alvarez ended the awed silence. 'What did he do with the pie?'

'Ate it,' said Dominick glumly. 'Had a perfectly good piece of his own, that he didn't touch.' He popped a lozenge into his mouth.

Alvarez shook his head. 'Not typical. His pattern is strictly submissive. I don't like it.'

'That's what I told Carver. But he was livid. Shaking. We all sat there until he escorted his wife to her room and came back. Then we had an interrogation. All we could get out of George was, "I thought I was panga to her."'

Alvarez shifted impatiently in his chair, reaching automatically for a bunch of grapes from the bowl on the desk. He was a small, spare man, and he felt defensive about it. 'Now what is all this panga business?' he demanded.

Womrath snorted, and began to peel a banana.

'Panga,' said Dominick, 'would appear to be some kind of complicated authority-submission relationship that exists among the gorgons.' Alvarez sat up straighter. 'They never mentioned it to us, because we never asked. Now it turns out to be crucial.' Dominick sighed. 'Fourteen months, just getting a three-man base down on the planet. Seven more to get the elders' permission to bring a gorgon here experimentally. All according to the book. We picked the biggest and brightest-looking one we could find: that was George. He seemed to be coming along great. And now this.'

'Well, chief,' said Womrath carefully, 'nobody has any more admiration than I have for Mrs. Carver as a consumer—she really puts it away, but it seems to me the question is, is *George* damaged——'

Dominick was shaking his head. 'I haven't told you the rest of it. This panga thing stopped Carver cold, but not for long. He beamed down to the planethead and had Rubinson ask the elders. "Is George panga to the Commandant's wife?"'

Alvarez grinned mirthlessly and clicked his tongue.

'Sure,' Dominick nodded. 'Who knows what a question like that may have meant to them? They answered back, in effect, "Certainly not," and wanted to know the details. Carver *told* them.'

'And?' said Alvarez.

'They said George was a shocking criminal who should be appropriately punished. Not by them, you understand—by us, because we're the offended parties. Moreover—now this must make sense to their peculiar way of looking at things—if *we* don't punish George to their satisfaction, *they'll* punish Rubinson and his whole crew.'

'How?' Alvarez demanded.

'By doing,' Dominick said, 'whatever it is we should have done to George—and that could be anything.'

Womrath pursed his lips to whistle, but no sound came out. He swallowed a mouthful of banana and tried again. Still nothing.

'You get it?' said Dominick with suppressed emotion. They all looked through the open doorway at George, squatting patiently in the other room. 'There's no trouble about "punishment"—we all know what it means, we've read the books. But how do you punish an alien like that? *An eye for a what?*'

'Now let's see if we have this straight,' said Dominick, sorting through the papers in his hand. Womrath and Alvarez looked on from either side. George tried to peek, too, but his photoceptors were too short. They were all standing in the outer office, which had been stripped to the bare walls and floor. 'One. We know a gorgon changes color according to his emotional state. When they're contented, they're a kind of rose pink. When they're unhappy, they turn blue.'

'He's been pink ever since we've had him on the Satellite,' said Womrath, glancing down at the gorgon.

'Except at the banquet,' Dominick answered thoughtfully. 'I remember he turned bluish just before . . . If we could find out what it was that set him off—— Well, first things first.' He held down another finger. 'Two, we don't have any information at all about local systems of reward and punishment. They may cut each other into bits for spitting on the side-

47

walk, or they may just slap each other's—um, wrists——' He looked unhappily down at George, all his auricles and photoceptors out on stalks.

'—for arson, rape and mopery,' Dominick finished. 'We don't know; we'll have to play it by ear.'

'What does George say about it?' Alvarez asked. 'Why don't you ask him?'

'We thought of that,' Womrath said glumly. 'Asked him what the elders would do to him in a case like this, and he said they'd quabble his infarcts, or something.'

'A dead end,' Dominick added. 'It would take us years . . .' He scrubbed his naked scalp with a palm. 'Well, number three, we've got all the furniture out of here—it's going to be damned crowded, with the whole staff working in my office, but never mind . . . Number four, there's his plate with the bread and water. And number five, that door has been fixed so it latches on the outside. Let's give it a dry run.' He led the way to the door; the others followed, including George. 'No, you stay in here,' Womrath told him. George stopped, blushing an agreeable pink.

Dominick solemnly closed the door and dropped the improvised latch into its socket. He punched the door button, found it satisfactorily closed. Through the transparent upper pane, they could see George inquisitively watching.

Dominick opened the door again. 'Now, George,' he said, 'pay attention. This is a *prison*. You're being *punished*. We're going to keep you in here, with nothing to eat but what's there, until we think you're punished enough. Understand?'

'Yes,' said George doubtfully.

'All right,' said Dominick, and closed the door. They all stood watching for a while, and George stood watching them back, but nothing else happened. 'Let's go into my office and wait,' said Dominick with a sigh. 'Can't expect miracles, all at once.'

They trooped down the corridor to the adjoining room and ate peanuts for a while. 'He's a sociable creature,' Womrath said hopefully. 'He'll get lonesome after a while.'

'And hungry,' Alvarez said. 'He never turns down a meal.'

Half an hour later, when they looked in, George was

48

thoughtfully chewing up the carpet. 'No, no, no, *no*, George,' said Dominick, bursting in on him. 'You're not supposed to eat anything except what we give you. This is a *prison*.'

'Good carpet,' said George, hurt.

'I don't care if it is. You don't eat it, understand?'

'Okay,' said George cheerfully. His color was an honest rose pink.

Four hours later, when Alvarez went off shift, George had settled down in a corner and pulled in all his appendages. He was asleep. If anything, he looked pinker that ever.

When Alvarez came on shift again, there was no doubt about it. George was sitting in the middle of the room, photoceptors out and waving rhythmically; his color was a glowing pink, the pink of a rose pearl. Dominick kept him in there for another day, just to make sure; George seemed to lose a little weight on the austere diet, but glowed a steady pink. He liked it.

II

Goose Kelly, the games instructor, tried to keep up a good front, but he had the worst case of wheel fever on SAPS 3107A. It had got so that looking out of that fat, blue-green planet, swimming there so close, was more than he could bear. Kelly was a big man, an outdoorman by instinct; he longed for natural air in his lungs, and turf under his feet. To compensate, he strode faster, shouted louder, got redder of face and bulgier of eye, bristled more fiercely. To quiet an occasional trembling of his hands, he munched sedative pills. He had dreams of falling, with which he bored the ship's Mother Hubbard and the Church of Marx padre by turns.

'Is that it?' he asked now, disapprovingly. He had never seen the gorgon before; Semantics, Medical and Xenology Sections had been keeping him pretty much to themselves.

Dominick prodded the pinkish sphere with his toe. 'Wake up, George.'

After a moment, the gorgon's skin became lumpy at half a dozen points. The lumps grew slowly into long, segmented stems. Some of these expanded at the tips into 'feet' and 'hands'; others flowered into the intricate patterns of auricles and photoceptors—and one speech organ, which looked like a small trumpet. 'Hello,' said George cheerfully.

'He can pull them back in any time?' Kelly asked, rubbing his chin.

'Yes. Show him, George.'

'All right.' The feather stalks became blank-tipped, then rapidly shrank, segment by segment. In less than two seconds, George was a smooth sphere again.

'Well, that makes for a little problem here,' said Kelly. 'You see what I mean? If you can't get a grip on him, how are you going to *punish* him like you say?'

'We've tried everything we could think of,' said Dominick. 'We locked him up, kept him on short rations, didn't talk to him ... He doesn't draw any pay, you know, so you can't fine him.'

'Or downgrade him on the promotion lists, either,' said Womrath gloomily.

'No. And it's a little late to use the Pavlov-Morganstern treatments we all had when we were children. We can't prevent a crime he's already committed. So our thought was, since you're the games instructor——'

'We thought,' Womrath said diplomatically, 'you might have noticed something that might be useful. You know, rough-housing and so on.'

Kelly thought this over. 'Well, there's low blows,' he said, 'but I mean, hell——' He gestured futilely at George, who had just decided to put his auricles out again. 'What would you——'

'No, that's out of the question,' Dominick said heavily. 'Well, I'm sorry, Kelly. It was nice of you to help out.'

'No, now, wait a minute,' said Kelly. 'I got something coming to me, maybe.' He nibbled a thumbnail, staring down at the gorgon. 'How would this be. I was thinking—sometimes the boys in the pool, they get kind of frisky, they take to ducking each other. Under the water. Now what I was thinking, he breathes air, doesn't he? You know what I mean?'

Dominick and Womrath looked at each other. 'It sounds possible,' said Dominick.

'Out of the question. We don't know what his tolerance is.

Suppose Kelly should damage him severely, or even——'

'Oh,' said Dominick. 'No, you're right, we couldn't take a chance.'

'I've been a games instructor for seventy-three years—two rejuvenations——' Kelly began, bristling.

'No, it isn't that, Kelly,' said Womrath hastily. 'We're just thinking, George isn't human. So how do we know how he'd react to a ducking?'

'On the other hand,' Dominick said, 'gorgons *do* turn blue when they're not happy—we have Rubinson's assurance for that. It seems to me George wouldn't be happy when smothering; that would be the whole point, wouldn't it? Dr. Alvarez would supervise closely, of course. Really, Alvarez, I don't see why not. Kelly, if you'll tell what time would be most convenient for you——'

'Well,' said Kelly, looking at his thumbwatch, 'hell, the pool is empty now—it's ladies' day, but all the girls are down in Section Seven, hanging around Mrs. Carver. I hear she's still hysterical.'

Struck by a thought, Alvarez was bending over to speak to the gorgon. 'George, you breathe by spiracles, is that correct? Those little tubes all over your skin?'

'Yes,' said George.

'Well, do they work under water?'

'No.'

Dominick and Kelly were listening with interest.

'If we held you under water, would it hurt you?'

George flickered uncertainly, from rose to pale magenta. 'Don't know. Little bit.'

The three men leaned closer. 'Well, George,' said Dominick tensely, 'would that be a *punishment*?'

George flickered again, violently. 'Yes. No. Maybe. Don't know.'

They straightened again, disappointed; Dominick sighed gustily. 'He always gives us those mixed-up answers. *I* don't know. Let's try it—what else can we do?'

Kelly found himself paired off with George, following Dominick and Dr. Alvarez, and preceding Womrath and an

51

orderly named Josling who was wheeling one of the dispensary pul-motors. The up-curving corridors were deserted. Kelly lagged a little, adjusting his pace to George's waddling steps. After a moment, he was surprised to feel something small and soft grip his fingers. He looked down; George the gorgon had put one seven-fingered 'hand' into his. The gorgon's flower-like photoceptors were turned trustfully upward.

Kelly was taken by surprise. No children were allowed on the Satellite, but Kelly had been the father of eight in a pre-vious rejuvenation. The confiding touch stirred old memories. 'That'll be all right,' said Kelly gruffly. 'You just come along with me.'

The pool, as he had predicted, was empty. Ripples reflected faint threads of light up the walls. 'The shallow end would be better,' said Kelly. His voice was hollow, and echoed back flatly. Pausing to peel off his coverall, he led George carefully down the steps into the pool. Half submerged, George floated. Kelly drew him gently out into deeper water.

Dominick and the others arranged themselves along the brink in interested attitudes. Kelly cleared his throat. 'Well,' he said, 'the way it generally happens, one of the boys will grab ahold of another one, like this——' He put his hands on the smooth floating globe, and hesitated.

'Go ahead now, Kelly,' called Dominick. 'Remember, you have a direct order to do this.'

'Sure,' said Kelly. 'Well——' he turned to the gorgon. 'Hold your breath now!' He pressed downward. The gorgon seemed lighter than he had expected, like an inflated ball; it was hard to force it under.

Kelly pushed harder. George went under briefly and slipped out of Kelly's hands, bobbing to the surface. The gorgon's speaking trumpet cleared itself of water with a *phonk* and said, 'Nice. Do again, Kelly.'

Kelly glanced over at Dominick, who said, 'Yes. Again.' Dr. Alvarez stroked his thin beard and said nothing.

Kelly took a deep sympathetic breath, and shoved the gorgon under. A few bubbles came to the surface; George's speaking trumpet broke water, but made no sound. Down be-low, Kelly could see his own pale hands gripping the gorgon's body; the water made them look bloodless; but not George; he was a clear, unblemished pink.

There was a discouraged silence when Kelly brought him back up.

'Listen,' said Dominick, 'I've got another idea. George, can you breathe through that speaking trumpet, too?'

'Yes,' said George cheerfully.

There was a chorus of disgusted 'Oh, wells.' Everybody brightened perceptibly. Josling polished his pul-motor with a rag. 'Go ahead, Kelly,' said Dominick. 'And this time, you hold him under.'

George went down for the third time. The bubbles swirled upward. The gorgon's speaking trumpet swayed toward the surface, but Kelly leaned farther over, blocking it with his forearm. After a moment, all of George's appendages began to contract. Kelly craned his neck downward anxiously. Was a hint of blue beginning to show?

'Keep him down,' said Alvarez sharply.

George was a blank sphere again. Then one or two of the limbs began to reappear; but they looked different somehow.

'Now?' said Kelly.

'Give him a second more,' said Dominick, leaning over precariously. 'It seems to me——'

Kelly's back muscles were knotted with tension. He did not like the way George's new limbs seemed to be flattening out, trailing limply—it was as if something had gone wrong in the works.

'I'm bringing him up,' he said hoarsely.

To Kelly's horror, when he lifted his hands. George stayed where he was. Kelly made a grab for him, but the gorgon slipped out from under his fingers. The new limbs stiffened and sculled vigorously; George darted away, deep under the water.

Leaning, open-mouthed, Dominick slipped and went into the pool with a majestic splash. He floundered and rose up, a moment later, streaming with water like a sea lion. Kelly, wading anxiously toward him, stopped when he saw that Dominick was safe. Both men looked down. Between them and

53

around them swam George, darting and drifting by turns, as much at home in the pool as a speckled trout.

'Fins!' said Dominick, stack-jawed. 'And *gills!*'

It may as well be said that Dr. Walter Alvarez was a misanthrope. He did not like people; he liked diseases. Down there on Planet Seven, once the trade mission was established, he could confidently expect enough new and startling ailments to keep him happy as a lark for years. Up here, all he got was sprained ankles, psychosomatic colds, hives and indigestion. There was one cook's helper named Samuels who kept coming back every Wednesday with the same boil on the back of his neck. It got so that in spite of himself, Alvarez spent the whole week dreading Wednesday. When he saw Samuels's earnest face coming through the door, something seemed to wind itself a little tighter inside him.

Some day, when Samuels opened his mouth to say. 'Hey, Doc——' Samuels always called him 'Doc'—the something inside him was going to break with a sound like a banjo string. What would happen then, Dr. Alvarez was unable to imagine.

When the gorgon had first been brought up to the Satellite, there had been two or three delightful little fungus infections, then nothing. A great disappointment. Alvarez had isolated and cultured almost a hundred microörganisms found in smears he had taken from George, but they were all nonviable in human tissue. The viable bacteria, viruses, parasites that always turned up on a life-infested planet, were evidently lurking in some organism other than the gorgons. They swam, at night, across the optical field of Dr. Alvarez's dreaming mind —rod-shaped ones, lens-shaped ones, wriggly ones, leggy ones and ones with teeth.

One morning Dr. Alvarez awoke with a desperate resolve. It was a Tuesday. Alvarez went directly to the infirmary, relieved Nurse Trumble, who was on duty, and, opening a locked cabinet, filled a hypodermic from an ampule of clear straw-colored fluid. The trade name of this substance was Betsoff; it was a counter-inhibitant which stunned the censor areas of the forebrain chiefly affected by the Pavlov-Morganstern treatments. (By an odd coincidence, the patentee was a Dr.

Jekyll.) Alvarez injected two c.c.'s of it directly into the median basilic vein and sat down to wait.

After a few minutes his perpetual bad humor began to lift. He felt a pleasant ebullience; the colors of things around him seemed brighter and clearer. 'Ha!' said Alvarez. He got up and went to his little refrigerator, where, after some search, he found half a dozen of the cultures he had made of microörganisms taken from gorgon smears. They were quiescent, of course—deep-frozen. Alvarez warmed them cautiously and added nutrients. All morning, while the usual succession of minor complaints paraded through the infirmary, the cultures grew and multiplied. Alvarez was jovial with his patients; he cracked a joke or two, and handed out harmless pills all around.

By noon, four of the cultures were flourishing. Alvarez carefully concentrated them into one, and loaded another hypodermic with the resulting brew. To his liverated intelligence, the matter was clear: No organism, man or pig or gorgon, was altogether immune to the microbes it normally carried in its body. Upset the balance by injecting massive colonies of any one of them, and you were going to have a sick gorgon—i.e. Alvarez thought, a punished gorgon.

The treatment might also kill the patient, but Alvarez lightheartedly dismissed this argument as a quibble. (Or quabble?) Armed with his hypo, he went forth looking for George.

He found him in the small assembly room, together with Dominick, Womrath, and a mechanic named Bob Ritner. They were all standing around a curious instrument, or object of art, built out of bar aluminum. 'It's a rack,' Ritner explained proudly. 'I saw a picture of it once in a kid's book.'

The chief feature of the 'rack' was a long, narrow table, with a windlass at one end. It looked like a crude device for stretching something.

'We thought the time had come for stern measures,' Dominick said, mopping his head.

'In the olden days,' Ritner put in, 'they used these on the prisoners when they wouldn't talk.'

'I talk,' said George unexpectedly.

'It's another punishment, George,' Dominick explained

55

kindly. 'Well, Alvarez, before we go ahead, I suppose you want to examine your patient.'

'Yes, just so, ha ha!' said Alvarez. He knelt down and peered keenly at George, who swiveled his photoceptors interestedly around to stare back. The doctor prodded George's hide; it was firm and resilient. The gorgon's color was a clear pink; the intricate folds of his auricles seemed crisp and alert.

Alvarez took a hand scale from his kit; it was preset for A-level gravity. 'Climb up here, George.' Obediently, the gorgon settled himself on the pan of the scale while Alvarez held it up. 'Hm,' said Alvarez. 'He's lost a good deal of weight.'

'He has?' asked Dominick hopefully.

'But he seems to be in unusually good condition—better than a week ago, I would say. Perhaps just a little sugar solution to pep him up——' Alvarez withdrew the hypo from his kit, aimed it at George's smooth skin and pressed the trigger.

Dominick sighed. 'Well, I suppose we might as well go ahead. George, just hop up there and let Ritner tie those straps onto you.'

George obediently climbed onto the table. Ritner buckled straps around four of his limbs and then began to tighten the cylinder. 'Not too much,' said George anxiously.

'I'll be careful,' Ritner assured him. He kept on winding the cylinder up. 'How does that feel?' George's 'arms' and 'legs' were half again their usual length, and still stretching.

'Tickles,' said George.

Ritner went on turning the handle. Womrath coughed nervously and was shushed. George's limbs kept on getting longer; then his body started to lengthen visibly.

'Are you all right, George?' Dominick asked.

'All right.'

Ritner gave the handle a last despairing twist. George's elongated body stretched all the way in comfort from one end of the rack to the other: there was no place else for him to go. 'Nice,' said George. 'Do again.' He was glowing a happy pink.

Ritner, who seemed about to cry, petulantly kicked his machine. Alvarez snorted and went away. In the corridor, unseen, he jumped up and clicked his heels together. He was having a wonderful time; his only regret was that it was not tomorrow. Come to think of it, why wait till Wednesday?

Commandant Charles Watson Carver, S.S., had been trained to make quick and courageous decisions. Once you began to entertain a doubt of your own rightness, you would hesitate too much, begin to second-guess yourself, fall prey to superstition and anxiety, and end up without any power of decision at all.

The trouble was, you could never be right all the time. Following the book to the letter, or improvising brilliantly, either way, you were bound to make mistakes. The thing was, to cross them off and go ahead just the same.

Carver firmed his chin and straightened his back, looking down at the sick gorgon. It was sick, all right, there was no question about that: the thing's limbs drooped and weaved slightly, dizzily. Its hide was dry and hot to the touch. 'How long has he been like this?' Carver demanded, hesitating only slightly over the 'he': aliens were 'it' to him and always had been, but it didn't do to let anybody know it.

'Twenty minutes, more or less,' said Dr. Nasalroad. 'I just got here myself'—he stifled a yawn—'about ten minutes ago.'

'What are you doing here, anyway?' Carver asked him. 'It's Alvarez's shift.'

Nasalroad looked embarrassed. 'I know. Alvarez is in the hospital, as a patient. I think he assaulted a cook's helper named Samuels—poured soup over his head. He was shouting something about boiling the boil on Samuel's neck. We had to put him under sedation; it took three of us.'

Carver set his jaw hard. 'Nasalroad, what in thunder is happening on this wheel, anyhow? First this thing attacks my wife—then Alvarez——' He glared down at George. 'Can you pull him out of this, whatever it is?'

Nasalroad looked surprised. 'That would be a large order. We don't know any gorgon medicine—I was assuming you'd want to beam down and ask *them*.'

That was reasonable, of course: the only hitch was, as usual, a matter of interpretation. Was this something they had negligently allowed to happen to an important alien representative, or was it the necessary and proper punishment they had all been looking for? Carver glanced at his thumbwatch: it was just about three hours before the elders' deadline.

He asked Nasalroad, 'What color would you say he is now? Not pink, certainly.'

'No-o. But not blue, either. I'd call it a kind of violet.'

'Hm. Well, anyhow, he's got smaller than he was, isn't that right? *Conspicuously* smaller.'

Nasalroad admitted it.

Carver made his decision. 'Do the best you can,' he said to Nasalroad. He lifted his wristcom, said briskly, 'Have you got a line-of-sight to the planethead?'

'*Yes, sir,*' the operator answered.

'All right, get me Rubinson.'

A few seconds passed. '*Planethead.*'

'Rubinson, this is Carver. Tell the elders we've got a pretty unhappy gorgon here. We're not sure just what did it—might have been any one of a lot of things—but he's lost a good deal of weight, and his color'—Carver hesitated—'it's bluish. Definitely *bluish*. Got that?'

'*Yes, chief. Thank goodness! I'll pass the message along right away, and call you back.*'

'Right.' Carver closed the wristcom with an assertive snap. The gorgon, when he glanced down at it, looked sicker than ever, but never mind. What happened to the gorgon was its lookout; Carver was doing his duty.

III

Alvarez awoke with a horrible headache and a sense of guilt. He was not in his own cubicle, but in one of the hospital bunks, dressed in a regulation set of hospital pajamas (with removable hood and gloves, capable of being converted into a spacesuit). He could just see the wall clock at the far end of the room. It was twenty-three hours—well into his shift. Alvarez scuttled out of bed, groaning, and looked at the chart beside it. *Mania, delusions. Sedation. Signed Nasalroad.*

Delusions: yes, he was having one now. He imagined he could remember heaving up a big tureen of mock-turtle soup over Samuels's startled face—splash, a smoking green torrent.

58

Good heavens! If that was *real*—Samuels! And the gorgon!

Groaning and lurching, Alvarez darted out of the room, past the orderly, Munch, who was sitting with a story viewer on his lap and couldn't get up fast enough. 'Dr. Alvarez! Dr. Nasalroad said——'

'Never mind Nasalroad,' he snapped, pawing in the refrigerator. He remembered those cultures being right back *there*: but now they were gone.

'—not to let you up until you acted normal again. Uh, how do you feel, Doctor?'

'I feel fine! What difference does that make? How is *he*?'

Munch looked puzzled and apprehensive. 'Samuels? Just superficial burns. We put him to bed in his own cubby, because——'

'Not Samuels!' Alvarez hissed, grabbing Munch by the front of his suit. 'The gorgon!'

'Oh, well, he's been sick, too. How did you know, though, Doctor? You were snoring when it happened. Listen, let go my suit, you're making me nervous.'

'Where?' Alvarez demanded, thrusting his scrawny face close to the other's.

'Where what? Oh, you mean the *gorgon*? Up in the little assembly room, the last I——'

Alvarez was gone, out the door and down the corridor like a small, bearded fireball. He found an anxious crowd assembled —Commandant and Mrs. Carver, Dominick and his staff, Urban and two assistants from Semantics, orderlies, porters, and Dr. Nasalroad. Nasalroad had the gaunt and bright-eyed appearance of a man who has been on wake-up pills too long. He started when he saw Alvarez.

'What's up?' Alvarez demanded, grabbing his sleeve. 'Where's the gorgon? What——'

'Be quiet,' said Nasalroad. 'George is over in that corner behind Carver. We're waiting for the delegation from planet-side. Rubinson said they were coming up, three of them with some kind of a box ...'

A loudspeaker said suddenly, 'I have the tender locked on.

59

Contact. Contact is made. The lock is opening; get ready, here they come.'

Alvarez couldn't see past Carver's bulk; he tried to get away, but Nasalroad stopped him. 'I want to *see*,' he said irritably.

'Listen,' Nasalroad said. 'I know what you did. I checked the Bets-off and those cultures against inventory. The gorgon seems to be recovering nicely, no thanks to you. Now has the stuff worn off you, or not? Because if not——'

A rustle went over the group. Alvarez and Nasalroad turned in time to see the door opening. Two large, vigorous-looking gorgons waddled through; they were carrying an enameled metal box between them. '*Foop!*' said the first one, experimentally. 'Where is gorgon George?'

'I'm all right,' Alvarez muttered. 'If I wasn't, I'd have done something uncivilised to you by now, wouldn't I?'

'I guess so,' said Nasalroad. They elbowed closer as the group shifted, making a space around the three gorgons. Peering, on tiptoe, Alvarez could see George standing shakily beside the other two. 'He looks terrible. Those are big ones, those other two, aren't they?'

'Not as big as George was when we got him,' Nasalroad muttered. 'Listen, Walt, if it turns out you've ruined the whole thing, I'll take a dose of Bets-off myself, and——'

'Listen!' snarled Alvarez. One of the gorgons was explaining. 'This is panga box. What you call? You know panga?'

'Well, uh, yes and no,' said Dominick uncomfortably. 'But what about the punishment? We understood——'

'Punishment later. You George, go in box.'

Obediently, George waddled over and squatted beside the mouth of the box. He bobbed uncertainly; he looked for all the world like a large woman trying to get into a small sports copter. There was a minor outbreak of nervous laughter, quickly suppressed.

George leaned, retracting most of his upper appendages. His round body began to be composed into a squarish shape, wedging itself into the box.

The other gorgons watched with an air of tension, photoceptors rigidly extended. A hush fell. Among the humans present there was a general air of Why-are-we-all-whispering?

George wriggled and oozed farther into the box. Momentarily he stuck. He flicked blue, then pink. His 'feet,' almost retracted, scrabbled feebly at the bottom of the box. Then he was in.

One of the other gorgons solemnly closed the lid on him and fastened it to make sure, then opened it again and helped him out. All three gorgons began to make rhythmic swaying motions with their 'arms' and other appendages. George, Alvarez thought, looked smug. He felt a sudden premonitory pang. What had he done?

'What's it all about?' Nasalroad demanded. 'Are they measuring him for a coffin, or——'

Dominick, overhearing, turned and said, 'I don't think so. Now this is interesting. You remember they said a panga box. What I'm afraid of is, they may have a standard of size. You see what I mean, they're measuring George to see if he falls below the minimum standard of, uh, panga relations.'

'Oh, heavens,' said another voice. It was Urban of Semantics, who had been neglected of late; they hadn't needed him since George learned English. He was peering over Dominick's shoulder, looking dumbfounded. He said, 'But don't you know the word we've been translating "elders" really means "smallest ones"? Good heavens——'

'I don't see——' Dominick began, but the Commandant's voice drowned him out. 'Quiet! Quiet please!' Carver was trumpeting. He went on, 'Our friends from Seven have an announcement to make. Now, then.'

To everyone's surprise, it was George who spoke, in the lisping accents of the gorgon language. No human present understood a word of it except Urban, who turned pale under his tan and began stammering inaudibly to himself.

One of the larger gorgons began to speak when George stopped. 'Most elder person, known to you by name George, wishes me to thank you all for kindness done him when he was humble youth.'

('Youth,' muttered Urban. 'But it really means "ungainly one"—or "fat boy"! Oh, my *heavens*!')

'Now that he has become an elder, it will be his most

pleasure to repay all kindness in agreeable legislative manner.'

('What does that mean?' Alvarez said aggrievedly. 'Why can't he talk for himself, anyway?'

'It would be beneath his dignity now,' said Nasalroad. 'Hush!')

'—*If*,' said the gorgon, 'you will succeed in giving elder person, known by name George, proper punishment as aforesaid.'

While the others stared with dumb dismay, Carver briskly snapped open his wristcom. 'Exactly how long have we got till that gorgon deadline is up?' he demanded.

There was a pause, while ears strained to catch the tiny voice.

'Just under half an hour.'

'This meeting will come to order!' said Carver, banging on the table. George and the other two gorgons were sitting opposite him, with the centerpiece of nasturtiums and ferns between them. Grouped around Carver were Dominick, Urban, Womrath, Alvarez, Nasalroad, Kelly and Ritner.

'Now this is the situation,' Carver said aggressively. 'This gorgon turns out to be a member of their ruling council, I don't understand why, but never mind that now—the point is, he's friendly disposed towards us, so we've succeeded in this mission *if* we can find that proper punishment—otherwise we're in the soup. Suggestions.'

(Dominick craned his bald head toward Alvarez across the table. 'Doctor, I had a thought,' he murmured. 'Would you say—is there anything peculiar about the gorgon's body constitution, as compared say to ours?'

'Certainly,' said Alvarez, dourly. 'Any number of things. You name it, they——')

Giving them a dirty look, Carver nodded to Ritner. 'Yes?'

'Well, I was thinking. I know the rack was a washout, but there was another thing they used to use, called the Iron Virgin. It had a door, like, with spikes on it——'

('What I had in mind,' Dominick said, 'is there anything that would tend to limit their body size—any danger or disadvantage in growing large?'

Alvarez frowned and looked at Nasalroad, who hitched his chair closer. 'The pressure——?' said Nasalroad tentatively. They rubbed their chins and looked at each other with professional glints in their eyes.

'What *about* the pressure?' Dominick prompted eagerly.)

'How long would it take you to build a thing like that?' Carver was asking Ritner.

'Well—ten, eleven hours.'

'Too long. That's out. Next!'

('They're actually a single cell—all colloidal fluid, at a considerable osmotic pressure. The bigger they get, the more pressure it takes to keep that shape. If they got too big, I rather imagine——'

Alvarez snapped his fingers, awed. 'They'd burst!')

Carver turned with an indignant glare. 'Gentlemen, if I could get a little cooperation out of you, instead of this continual distraction—— All right, Womrath?'

'Sir, I was just wondering, suppose if we let him turn into a fish, the way he did before in the pool—but then we'd net him and take him out of the water fast. That way, maybe——'

'It wouldn't work,' said Kelly. 'He changed back in about a second, the other time.'

Nobody was paying any attention to him. One of the big gorgons, who had been staring fixedly at the flowers in the middle of the table, had suddenly grabbed a handful and was stuffing them into his mouth. George said something shrill in gorgon talk, and snatched the flowers away again. The other gorgon looked abashed, but flushed pink.

George, on the other hand, was distinctly blue.

His 'hand,' clutching the mangled flowers, hesitated. Slowly, as if with an effort, he put them back in the bowl.

The other two gorgons twined their 'arms' around him. After a moment George looked more like his old self, but a hint of blue remained.

'What is it?' said Carver alertly. 'Did we do something, finally?' He snapped open his wristcom. 'There's still ten minutes before the deadline, so——'

'Did you turn blue because we punished you, George?' Womrath asked.

'No,' said George unexpectedly. 'Hard for me to be elder.'
He added a few words in his own language to the other
gorgons, and their 'arms' twined around him again. 'Before,
they panga to *me*,' added George.

('Then that's why he took the pie away from the Commandant's wife!' said Dominick, smiting himself on the forehead.

'Of course. They——')

'What's that? What's that?' Carver turned, bristling.

'Why, this explains that pie business,' said Dominick. 'He
felt protective towards your wife, you see—that's what
"panga" means. They none of them have much control over
their own appetites, so they guard each other. As they grow
older, and get more self-control, they're expected to get
smaller, not bigger. George felt confused about his panga
relationships to us, but in your wife's case, he was positive one
more mouthful would make her explode——'

Carver was red to the ears. 'Nonsense!' he shouted.
'Dominick, you're being insulting, insubordinate and un-
patriotic!'

George, looking on interestedly, piped a few words in the
gorgon language. One of the other gorgons immediately spoke
up: 'Elder person says, you with smooth head are a smart
man. He says, the other big one who talks too much is wrong.'

Carver's jaws worked. He looked at the gorgons, then
around the table. No one said anything.

Carver set his jaw heroically. 'Well, gentlemen,' he began,
'we certainly tried, but——'

'Wait a minute!' said Alvarez. Somewhere in his narrow
skull a great light had dawned. 'George, am I panga to
you?'

George's auricles weaved tensely. 'Yes,' he said. 'You very
small man.'

'Good,' said Alvarez, dry-washing his bony hands. 'And you
still have to be punished, for that mistake you made at the
banquet?'

George's speaking tube buzzed unhappily. 'Yes,' he said.

'All right,' said Alvarez. Everybody was looking at him,
with expressions varying from puzzlement to alarm. Alvarez

took a deep breath. 'Then here are my orders to you,' he said. '*Do as you please!*'

There was a hiss of indrawn breath from Urban. Most of the others looked at Alvarez as if he had grown snakes for hair. 'Doctor,' said Carver, 'have you gone off your——'

The chorus of gasps stopped him. Up on the table, flushing blue and bright pink by turns like a sky sign, George was gobbling up the flowers in the centerpiece. Next he ate the bowl. One of his flailing limbs raked in the scratch pad Urban had been doodling on. He ate that.

Next moment he was leaping to the floor, making Ritner duck wildly as he passed. Part of Dominick's detachable hood went with him, disappearing with hoarse munching sounds. With a gulp, George swallowed it and began on the carpet. He was eating greedily, frantically. The other two gorgons hovered around him with shrill gorgon cries, but he ate on, oblivious. Now he was bright blue and bulging, but still he ate.

'Stop it!' shouted Alvarez. 'George, *stop* that!'

George rocked to a halt. Gradually his blueness faded. The other gorgons were prodding and patting him anxiously. George looked all right, but it was obvious as he stood there that he would never fit into the panga box again.

He was as big as the other two; maybe a little bigger.

'Alvarez,' said Carver, wildly, 'why did you——'

'He was going to burst,' said Alvarez, twitching with excitement. 'Couldn't you tell? Another mouthful or two——'

Carver recovered himself. He straightened his coverall and thrust out his chin. 'At any rate,' he said, 'he was certainly blue that time. You all saw it—isn't that right?' He looked around triumphantly. 'And by heaven, it happened inside the time limit. So, unless I'm very much mistaken——'

One of the two attendant gorgons raised his photoceptors. It was hard to tell which was George, now, except that his color was still a little lavender. The other gorgon spoke two brief sentences in his own language, and then all three of them waddled off together toward the exit.

'What was that? What did he say?' demanded Carver.

Urban cleared his throat; he had turned pale again. 'He said you should get the tender ready to take them back home.'

'The tender is there,' said Carver indignantly, 'they can go back any time they want. But what did he say about the punishment?'

Urban cleared his throat again, looking bemused. 'They say the punishment is good. More severe than any they ever thought of, in twenty thousand years. They say they won't have to punish Rubinson and the others, now, because you have done all the punishment necessary.'

'Well?' said Carver. 'Why are you looking that way? What's the hitch? Are they going to refuse to enter the Union, after all this?'

'No,' said Urban. 'They say we are all panga to them now. They'll do as we say—let us land and build the distribution centers, start them consuming in massive quantity. . . .'

'But that'll destroy them!' someone interjected in a horrified tone.

'Oh, yes,' said Urban.

Carver sighed. He had been in the SAPS service most of his life and was proud of his record. He played it as a game; the new, virgin planets were the prizes, and he kept score with the row of tiny iridium buttons on his breast pocket. He said into his wristcom, 'Let me know when Rubinson and his crew are on the way up.'

There was a long wait. The silence grew oppressive. At length the wall screen lighted up with a view of Planet Seven, gilded along one cusp, blue-green and mysterious in the shadow. A silver spark was floating up out of the night side. *Here they come now,*' said the voice.

Carver sighed again. 'When they make contact,' he said, 'secure the tender and then signal for acceleration stations. We're leaving Seven—tell Mr. Fruman to set a first approximation for our next star of call.'

Alvarez, twitching and frowning, clutched at the front of his coverall. 'You're letting them go?' he demanded. 'Not landing on Seven—after all this work?'

Carver was staring into the view plate. 'Some things,' he said slowly and unwillingly, 'are not meant to be consumed.'

STRANGER STATION

THE clang of metal echoed hollowly down through the Station's many vaulted corridors and rooms. Paul Wesson stood listening for a moment as the rolling echoes died away. The maintenance rocket was gone, heading back to Home; they had left him alone in Stranger Station.

Stranger Station! The name itself quickened his imagination. Wesson knew that both orbital stations had been named a century ago by the then British administration of the satellite service; 'Home' because the larger, inner station handled the traffic of Earth and its colonies; 'Stranger' because the outer station was designed specifically for dealings with foreigners ... beings from outside the solar system. But even that could not diminish the wonder of Stranger Station, whirling out here alone in the dark—waiting for its once-in-two-decades visitor....

One man, out of all Sol's billions, had the task and privilege of enduring the alien's presence when it came. The two races, according to Wesson's understanding of the subject, were so fundamentally different that it was painful for them to meet. Well, he had volunteered for the job, and he thought he could handle it—the rewards were big enough.

He had gone through all the tests, and against his own expectations he had been chosen. The maintenance crew had brought him up as dead weight, drugged in a survival hamper; they had kept him the same way while they did their work, and then had brought him back to consciousness. Now they were gone. He was alone.

... But not quite.

'Welcome to Stranger Station, Sergeant Wesson,' said a pleasant voice. 'This is your alpha network speaking. I'm here to protect and serve you in every way. If there's anything you want, just ask me.' It was a neutral voice, with a kind of professional friendliness in it, like that of a good schoolteacher or rec supervisor.

Wesson had been warned, but he was still shocked at the human quality of it. The alpha networks were the last word in robot brains—computers, safety devices, personal servants, libraries, all wrapped up in one, with something so close to 'personality' and 'free will' that experts were still arguing the question. They were rare and fantastically expensive; Wesson had never met one before.

'Thanks,' he said now, to the empty air. 'Uh—what do I call you, by the way? I can't keep saying, "Hey, alpha network." '

'One of your recent predecessors called me Aunt Nettie,' was the response.

Wesson grimaced. Alpha network—Aunt Nettie. He hated puns; that wouldn't do. 'The aunt part is all right,' he said. 'Suppose I call you Aunt Jane. That was my mother's sister; you sound like her, a little bit.'

'I am honored,' said the invisible mechanism politely. 'Can I serve you any refreshments now? Sandwiches? A drink?'

'Not just yet,' said Wesson. 'I think I'll look the place over first.'

He turned away. That seemed to end the conversation as far as the network was concerned. A good thing; it was all right to have it for company, speaking when spoken to, but if it got talkative. . . .

The human part of the Station was in four segments: bedroom, living room, dining room, bath. The living room was comfortably large and pleasantly furnished in greens and tans: the only mechanical note in it was the big instrument console in one corner. The other rooms, arranged in a ring around the living room, were tiny; just enough space for Wesson, a narrow encircling corridor, and the mechanisms that would serve him. The whole place was spotlessly clean, gleaming and efficient in spite of its twenty-year layoff.

This is the gravy part of the run, Wesson told himself. The month before the alien came—good food, no work, and an alpha network for conversation. 'Aunt Jane, I'll have a small steak now,' he said to the network. 'Medium rare, with hashed

68

brown potatoes, onions and mushrooms, and a glass of lager. Call me when it's ready.'

'Right,' said the voice pleasantly. Out in the dining room, the autochef began to hum and cluck self-importantly. Wesson wandered over and inspected the instrument console. Airlocks were sealed and tight, said the dials; the air was cycling. The Station was in orbit, and rotating on its axis with a force at the perimeter, where Wesson was, of one g. The internal temperature of this part of the Station was an even 73°.

The other side of the board told a different story; all the dials were dark and dead. Sector Two, occupying a volume some eighty-eight thousand times as great as this one, was not yet functioning.

Wesson had a vivid mental image of the Station, from photographs and diagrams—a five-hundred-foot duralumin sphere, onto which the shallow thirty-foot disk of the human section had been stuck apparently as an afterthought. The whole cavity of the sphere, very nearly—except for a honeycomb of supply and maintenance rooms, and the all-important, recently enlarged vats—was one cramped chamber for the alien. . . .

'Steak's ready!' said Aunt Jane.

The steak was good, bubbling crisp outside the way he liked it, tender and pink inside. 'Aunt Jane,' he said with his mouth full, 'this is pretty soft, isn't it?'

'The steak?' asked the voice, with a faintly anxious note.

Wesson grinned. 'Never mind,' he said. 'Listen, Aunt Jane, you've been through this routine—how many times? Were you installed with the Station, or what?'

'I was not installed with the Station,' said Aunt Jane primly. 'I have assisted at three contacts.'

'Um. Cigarette,' said Wesson, slapping his pockets. The autochef hummed for a moment, and popped a pack of G.I.'s out of a vent. Wesson lit up. 'All right,' he said, 'you've been through this three times. There are a lot of things you can tell me, right?'

'Oh, yes, certainly. What would you like to know?'

Wesson smoked, leaning back reflectively, green eyes narrowed. 'First,' he said, 'read me the Pigeon report—you

69

know, from the *Brief History*. I want to see if I remember it right.'

'Chapter Two,' said the voice promptly. 'First contact with a non-Solar intelligence was made by Commander Ralph C. Pigeon on July 1, 1987, during an emergency landing on Titan. The following is an excerpt from his official report:

' "While searching for a possible cause for our mental disturbance, we discovered what appeared to be a gigantic construction of metal on the far side of the ridge. Our distress grew stronger with the approach to this construction, which was polyhedral and approximately five times the length of the *Cologne*.

' "Some of those present expressed a wish to retire, but Lt. Acuff and myself had a strong sense of being called or summoned in some indefinable way. Although our uneasiness was not lessened, we therefore agreed to go forward and keep radio contact with the rest of the party while they returned to the ship.

' "We gained access to the alien construction by way of a large, irregular opening.... The internal temperature was minus seventy-five degrees Fahrenheit; the atmosphere appeared to consist of methane and ammonia.... Inside the second chamber, an alien creature was waiting for us. We felt the distress which I have tried to describe, to a much greater degree than before, and also the sense of summoning or pleading.... We observed that the creature was exuding a thick yellowish fluid from certain joints or pores in its surface. Though disgusted, I managed to collect a sample of this exudate, and it was later forwarded for analysis...."

'The second contact was made ten years later by Commodore Crawford's famous Titan Expedition——'

'No, that's enough,' said Wesson. 'I just wanted the Pigeon quote.' He smoked, brooding. 'It seems kind of chopped off, doesn't it. Have you got a longer version in your memory banks anywhere?'

There was a pause. 'No,' said Aunt Jane.

'There was more to it when I was a kid,' Wesson complained nervously. 'I read that book when I was twelve, and I remember a long description of the alien ... that is, I remember its being there.' He swung around. 'Listen, Aunt Jane —you're a sort of universal watchdog, that right? You've got cameras and mikes all over the Station?'

'Yes,' said the network, sounding—was it Wesson's imagination?—faintly injured.

'Well, what about Sector Two—you must have cameras up there, too, isn't that so?'

'Yes.'

'All right, then you can tell me. What do the aliens look like?'

There was a definite pause. 'I'm sorry, I can't tell you that,' said Aunt Jane.

'No,' said Wesson, 'I didn't think you could. You've got orders not to, I guess, for the same reason those history books have been cut since I was a kid. Now, what would the reason be? Have you got any idea, Aunt Jane?'

There was another pause. 'Yes,' the voice admitted.

'Well?'

'I'm sorry, I can't——'

'—tell you that,' Wesson repeated along with it. 'All right. At least we know where we stand.'

'Yes, Sergeant. Would you like some dessert?'

'No dessert. One other thing. *What happens to Station watchmen, like me, after their tour of duty?*'

'They are upgraded to Class Seven, students with unlimited leisure, and receive outright gifts of seven thousand stellors, plus free Class One housing....'

'Yeah, I know all that,' said Wesson, licking his dry lips. 'But here's what I'm asking you. The ones you know—what kind of shape were they in when they left here?'

'The usual human shape,' said the voice brightly. 'Why do you ask, Sergeant?'

Wesson made a discontented gesture. 'Something I remember from a bull session at the Academy. I can't get it out of my head; I know it had something to do with the Station. Just part of a sentence—"blind as a bat, and white bristles all over." Now, would that be a description of the alien ... or the watchman when they came to take him away?'

Aunt Jane went into one of her heavy pauses. 'All right, I'll save you the trouble,' said Wesson. 'You're sorry, you can't tell me that.'

'I *am* sorry,' said the robot, sincerely.

As the slow days passed into weeks, Wesson grew aware of the Station almost as a living thing. He could feel its resilient metal ribs enclosing him, lightly bearing his weight with its own as it swung. He could feel the waiting emptiness 'up there' and he sensed the alert electronic network that spread around him everywhere, watching and probing, trying to anticipate his needs.

Aunt Jane was a model companion. She had a record library of thousands of hours of music; she had films to show him, and micro-printed books that he could read on the scanner in the living room; or if he preferred, she would read to him. She controlled the Station's three telescopes, and on request would give him a view of Earth, or the Moon, or Home. . . .

But there was no news. Aunt Jane would obligingly turn on the radio receiver if he asked her, but nothing except static came out. That was the thing that weighed most heavily on Wesson, as time passed: the knowledge that radio silence was being imposed on all ships in transit, on the orbital stations, and on the planet-to-space transmitters. It was an enormous, almost a crippling handicap. Some information could be transmitted over relatively short distances by photophone, but ordinarily the whole complex traffic of the spacelanes depended on radio.

But this coming alien contact was so delicate a thing that even a radio voice, out here where the Earth was only a tiny disk twice the size of the Moon, might upset it. It was so precarious a thing, Wesson thought, than only one man could be allowed in the Station while the alien was there, and to give that man the company that would keep him sane, they had to install an alpha network. . . .

'Aunt Jane?'

The voice answered promptly, 'Yes, Paul?'

'This distress that the books talk about—you wouldn't know what it is, would you?'

'No, Paul.'

'Because robot brains don't feel it, right?'

'Right, Paul.'

'So tell me this—why do they need a man here at all? Why can't they get along with just you?'

A pause. 'I don't know, Paul.' The voice sounded faintly wistful. Were those gradations of tone really in it, Wesson wondered, or was his imagination supplying them?

He got up from the living room couch and paced restlessly back and forth. 'Let's have a look at Earth,' he said. Obediently, the viewing screen on the console glowed into life: there was the blue Earth, swimming deep below him, in its first quarter, jewel bright. 'Switch it off,' Wesson said.

'A little music?' suggested the voice, and immediately began to play something soothing, full of woodwinds.

'No,' said Wesson. The music stopped.

Wesson's hands were trembling; he had a caged and frustrated feeling.

The fitted suit was in its locker beside the air lock. Wesson had been topside in it once or twice; there was nothing to see up there, just darkness and cold. But he had to get out of this squirrel cage. He took the suit down and began to get into it.

'Paul,' said Aunt Jane anxiously, 'are you feeling nervous?'

'Yes,' he snarled.

'Then don't go into Sector Two,' said Aunt Jane.

'Don't tell me what to do, you hunk of tin!' said Wesson with sudden anger. He zipped up the front of his suit with a vicious motion.

Aunt Jane was silent.

Seething, Wesson finished his check-off and opened the lock door.

The air lock, an upright tube barely large enough for one man, was the only passage between Sector One and Sector Two. It was also the only exit from Sector One; to get here in the first place, Wesson had had to enter the big lock at the 'south' pole of the sphere, and travel all the way down inside, by drop hole and catwalk. He had been drugged unconscious at the time, of course. When the time came, he would go out the same way; neither the maintenance rocket nor the tanker had any space, or time, to spare.

At the 'north' pole, opposite, there was a third air lock, this one so huge it could easily have held an interplanet freighter. But that was nobody's business—no human being's.

In the beam of Wesson's helmet lamp, the enormous central cavity of the Station was an inky gulf that sent back only remote, mocking glimmers of light. The near walls sparkled with hoarfrost. Sector Two was not yet pressurised; there was only a diffuse vapor that had leaked through the airseal and had long since frozen into the powdery deposit that lined the walls. The metal rang cold under his shod feet; the vast emptiness of the chamber was the more depressing because it was airless, unwarmed and unlit. *Alone*, said his footsteps; *alone*. . . .

He was thirty yards up the catwalk when his anxiety suddenly grew stronger. Wesson stopped in spite of himself, and turned clumsily, putting his back to the wall. The support of the solid wall was not enough. The catwalk seemed threatening to tilt underfoot, dropping him into the lightless gulf.

Wesson recognized this drained feeling, this metallic taste at the back of his tongue. It was fear.

The thought ticked through his head, *They want me to be afraid*. But why? Why now? Of what?

Equally suddenly, he knew. The nameless pressure tightened like a great fist closing, and Wesson had the appalling sense of something so huge that it had no limits at all, descending, with a terrible endless swift slowness. . . .

It was time.

His first month was up.

The alien was coming.

As Wesson turned, gasping, the whole huge structure of the Station around him seemed to dwindle to the size of an ordinary room . . . and Wesson with it, so that he seemed to himself like a tiny insect, frantically scuttling down the walls toward safety.

Behind him as he ran, the Station *boomed*.

In the silent rooms, all the lights were burning dimly. Wesson lay still, looking at the ceiling. Up there his imagination formed a shifting, changing image of the alien—huge,

74

shadowy, formlessly menacing.

Sweat had gathered in globules on his brow. He stared unable to look away.

'That was why you didn't want me to go topside, huh, Aunt Jane?' he said hoarsely.

'Yes. The nervousness is the first sign. But you gave me a direct order, Paul.'

'I know it,' he said vaguely, still staring fixedly at the ceiling. 'A funny thing. . . . Aunt Jane?'

'Yes, Paul?'

'You won't tell me what it looks like, right?'

'*No*, Paul.'

'I don't want to know. Lord, I don't *want* to know. . . . Funny thing, Aunt Jane, part of me is just pure funk. I'm so scared I'm nothing but a jelly——'

'I know,' said the voice gently.

'——and part is real cool and calm, as if it didn't matter. Crazy, the things you think about. You know?'

'What things, Paul?'

He tried to laugh. 'I'm remembering a kid's party I went to twenty . . . twenty-five years ago. I was, let's see, I was nine. I remember, because that was the same year my father died.

'We were living in Dallas then, in a rented mobilehouse, and there was a family in the next tract with a bunch of red-headed kids. They were always throwing parties; nobody liked them much, but everybody always went.'

'Tell me about the party, Paul.'

He shifted on the couch. 'This one, this one was a Hal-lowe'en party. I remember the girls had on black and orange dresses, and boys mostly wore spirit costumes. I was about the youngest kid there, and I felt kind of out of place. Then all of a sudden one of the redheads jumps up in a skull mask, hollering, "C'mon, everybody get ready for hidenseek." And he grabs *me*, and says, "*You* be it," and before I can even move, he shoves me into a dark closet. And I hear that door lock behind me.'

He moistened his lips. 'And then—you know, in the dark-ness—I feel something hit my *face*. You know, cold and clammy, like, I don't know, something dead. . . .

75

'I just hunched up on the floor of that closet, waiting for that thing to touch me again. You know? That thing, cold and kind of gritty, hanging up there. You know what it was? A cloth glove, full of ice and bran cereal. A joke. Boy, that was one joke I never forgot.... Aunt Jane?'

'Yes, Paul.'

'Hey, I'll bet you alpha networks make great psychs, huh? I could lie here and tell you anything, because you're just a machine—right?'

'Right, Paul,' said the network sorrowfully.

'Aunt Jane, Aunt Jane.... It's no use kidding myself along. I can *feel* that thing up there, just a couple of yards away.'

'I know you can, Paul.'

'I can't stand it, Aunt Jane.'

'You can if you think you can, Paul.'

He writhed on the couch. 'It's—it's dirty, it's clammy. My God, is it going to be like that for *five months*? I can't, it'll kill me, Aunt Jane.'

There was another thunderous boom, echoing down through the structural members of the Station. 'What's that?' Wesson gasped. 'The other ship—casting off?'

'Yes. Now he's alone, just as you are.'

'Not like me. He can't be feeling what I'm feeling. Aunt Jane, you don't know....'

Up there, separated from him only by a few yards of metal, the alien's enormous, monstrous body hung. It was that poised weight, as real as if he could touch it, that weighed down his chest.

Wesson had been a space dweller for most of his adult life, and knew even in his bones that if an orbital station ever collapsed the 'under' part would not be crushed but would be hurled away by its own angular momentum. This was not the oppressiveness of planetside buildings, where the looming mass above you seemed always threatening to fall : this was something else, completely distinct, and impossible to argue away.

It was the scent of danger, hanging unseen up there in the dark, waiting, cold and heavy. It was the recurrent nightmare of Wesson's childhood—the bloated unreal shape, no-color, no-size, that kept on hideously falling toward his face. . . . It was the dead puppy he had pulled out of the creek, that summer in Dakota ... wet fur, limp head, cold, cold, *cold*. . . .

With an effort, Wesson rolled over on the couch and lifted himself to one elbow. The pressure was an insistent chill weight on his skull; the room seemed to dip and swing around him in slow, dizzy circles.

Wesson felt his jaw muscles contorting with the strain as he knelt, then stood erect. His back and legs tightened; his mouth hung painfully open. He took one step, then another, timing them to hit the floor as it came upright.

The right side of the console, the one that had been dark, was lighted. Pressure in Sector Two, according to the indicator was about one and a third atmospheres. The air-lock indicator showed a slightly higher pressure of oxygen and argon; that was to keep any of the alien atmosphere from contaminating Sector One, but it also meant that the lock would no longer open from either side. Wesson found that irrationally comforting.

'Lemme see Earth,' he gasped.

The screen lighted up as he stared into it. 'It's a long way down,' he said. A long, long way down to the bottom of that well. . . . He had spent ten featureless years as a servo tech in Home Station. Before that, he'd wanted to be a pilot, but had washed out the first year—couldn't take the math. But he had never once thought of going back to Earth.

Now, suddenly, after all these years, that tiny blue disk seemed infinitely desirable.

'Aunt Jane, Aunt Jane, it's beautiful,' he mumbled.

Down there, he knew, it was spring; and in certain places, where the edge of darkness retreated, it was morning: a watery blue morning like the sea light caught in an agate, a morning with smoke and mist in it; a morning of stillness and promise. Down there, lost years and miles away, some tiny dot of a woman was opening her microscopic door to listen to an atom's song. Lost, lost, and packed away in cotton wool, like a specimen slide: one spring morning on Earth.

Black miles above, so far that sixty Earths could have been piled one on another to make a pole for his perch, Wesson

77

swung in his endless circle within a circle. Yet, fast as the gulf beneath him was, all this—Earth, Moon, orbital stations, ships; yes, the Sun and all the rest of his planets, too—was the merest sniff of space, to be pinched up between thumb and finger.

Beyond—there was the true gulf. In that deep night, galaxies lay sprawled aglitter, piercing a distance that could only be named in a meaningless number, a cry of dismay: O, O, O....

Crawling and fighting, blasting with energies too big for them, men had come as far as Jupiter. But if a man had been tall enough to lie with his boots toasting in the Sun and his head freezing at Pluto, still he would have been too small for that overwhelming emptiness. Here, not at Pluto, was the outermost limit of man's empire: here the Outside funneled down to meet it, like the pinched waist of an hour-glass: here, and only here, the two worlds came near enough to touch. Ours—and Theirs.

Down at the bottom of the board, now, the golden dials were faintly alight, the needles trembling ever so little on their pins.

Deep in the vats, the vats, the golden liquid was trickling down: *'Though disgusted, I took a sample of the exudate and it was forwarded for analysis. . . .'*

Space-cold fluid, trickling down the bitter walls of the tubes, forming little pools in the cups of darkness; goldenly agleam there, half alive. The golden elixir. One drop of the concentrate would arrest aging for twenty years—keep you arteries soft, tonus good, eyes clear, hair pigmented, brain alert.

That was what the tests of Pigeon's sample had showed. That was the reason for the whole crazy history of the 'alien trading post'—first a hut on Titan, then later, when people understood more about the problem, Stranger Station.

Once every twenty years, an alien would come down out of Somewhere, and sit in the tiny cage we had made for him, and make us rich beyond our dreams—rich with life;—and still we did not know why.

Above him, Wesson imagined he could see that sensed body

78

a-wallow in the glacial blackness, its bulk passively turning with the station's spin, bleeding a chill gold into the lips of the tubes; drip, drop.

Wesson held his head. The pressure inside made it hard to think; it felt as if his skull were about to fly apart. 'Aunt Jane,' he said.

'Yes, Paul.' The kindly, comforting voice: like a nurse. The nurse who stands beside your cot while you have painful, necessary things done to you. Efficient, trained friendliness.

'Aunt Jane,' said Wesson, 'do you know why they keep coming back?'

'No,' said the voice precisely. 'It is a mystery.'

Wesson nodded. 'I had,' he said, 'an interview with Gower before I left Home. You know Gower? Chief of the Outerworld Bureau. Came up especially to see me.'

'Yes?' said Aunt Jane encouragingly.

'Said to me, "Wesson, you got to find out. Find out if we can count on them to keep up the supply. You know? There's fifty million more of us," he says, "than when you were born. We need more of the stuff, and we got to know if we can count on it. Because," he says, "you know what would happen if it stopped?" Do you know, Aunt Jane?'

'It would be,' said the voice, 'a catastrophe.'

'That's right,' Wesson said respectfully. 'It would. Like, he says to me, "What if the people in the Nefud area were cut off from the Jordan Valley Authority? Why, there'd be millions dying of thirst in a week.

'"Or what if the freighters stopped coming to Moon Base. Why," he says, "there'd be thousands starving and smothering to death."

'He says, "Where the water is, where you can get food and air, people are going to settle, and get married, you know? and have kids."

'He says, "If the so-called longevity serum stopped coming...." Says, "Every twentieth adult of the Sol family is due for his shot this year." Says, "Of those, almost twenty per cent are one hundred fifteen or older." Says, "The deaths in that group in the first year would be at least three times what the actuarial tables call for." ' Wesson raised a strained face. 'I'm

79

thirty-four, you know?' he said. 'That Gower, he made me feel like a baby.'

Aunt Jane made a sympathetic noise.

'Drip, drip,' said Wesson hysterically. The needles of the tall golden indicators were infinitesimally higher. 'Every twenty years we need more of the stuff, so somebody like me has to come out and take it for five lousy months. And one of *them* has to come out and sit there, and *drip. Why*, Aunt Jane? What for? Why should it matter to them whether we live a long time or not? Why do they keep on coming back? What do they take *away* from here?'

But to these questions, Aunt Jane had no reply.

All day and every day, the lights burned cold and steady in the circular gray corridor around the rim of Sector One. The hard gray flooring had been deeply scuffed in that circular path before Wesson ever walked there: the corridor existed for that only, like a treadmill in a squirrel cage; it said 'Walk,' and Wesson walked. A man would go crazy if he sat still, with that squirming, indescribable pressure on his head; and so Wesson paced off the miles, all day and every day, until he dropped like a dead man in the bed at night.

He talked, too, sometimes to himself, sometimes to the listening alpha network; sometimes it was difficult to tell which. 'Moss on a rock,' he muttered, pacing. 'Told him, wouldn't give twenty mills for any damn shell.... Little pebbles down there, all colors.' He shuffled on in silence for a while. Abruptly: 'I don't see *why* they couldn't have given me a cat.'

Aunt Jane said nothing. After a moment Wesson went on, 'Nearly everybody at Home has a cat, for God's sake, or a goldfish or something. You're all right, Aunt Jane, but I can't *see* you. My God, I mean if they couldn't send a man a woman for company, what I mean, my God, I never liked *cats*.' He swung around the doorway into the bedroom, and absent-mindedly slammed his fist into the bloody place on the wall.

'But a cat would have been *something*,' he said.

Aunt Jane was still silent.

'Don't pretend your damn feelings are hurt, I know you,

80

you're only a damn machine,' said Wesson. 'Listen, Aunt Jane, I remember a cereal package one time that had a horse and a cowboy on the side. There wasn't much room, so about all you saw was their faces. It used to strike me funny how much they looked alike. Two ears on the top with hair in the middle. Two eyes. Nose. Mouth with teeth in it. I was thinking, we're kind of distant cousins, aren't we, us and the horses. But compared to that thing up there—we're *brothers*. You know?'

'Yes,' said Aunt Jane, quietly.

'So I keep asking myself, why couldn't they have sent a horse, or a cat, *instead* of a man? But I guess the answer is because only a man could take what I'm taking. God, only a man. Right?'

'Right,' said Aunt Jane with deep sorrow.

Wesson stopped at the bedroom doorway again and shuddered, holding onto the frame. 'Aunt Jane,' he said in a low, clear voice, 'you take pictures of *him* up there, don't you?'

'Yes, Paul.'

'And you take pictures of me. And then what happens? After it's all over, who looks at the pictures?'

'I don't know,' said Aunt Jane humbly.

'You don't know. But whoever looks at 'em, it doesn't do any good. Right? We got to find out why, why, why.... And we never do find out, do we?'

'No,' said Aunt Jane.

'But don't they figure that if the man who's going through it could see him, he might be able to tell something? That other people couldn't? Doesn't that make sense?'

'That's out of my hands, Paul.'

He sniggered. 'That's funny. Oh, that's funny.' He chortled in his throat, reeling around the circuit.

'Yes, that's funny,' said Aunt Jane.

'Aunt Jane, tell me what happens to the watchmen.'

'... I can't tell you that, Paul.'

He lurched into the living room, sat down before the console, beat on its smooth, cold metal with his fists. 'What are you, some kind of monster? Isn't there any blood in your veins, damn it, or oil or *anything*?'

'Please, Paul——'

'Don't you see, all I want to know, can they talk? Can they tell anything after their tour is over?'

'. . . No, Paul.'

He stood upright, clutching the console for balance. 'They can't? No, I figured. And you know why?'

'No.'

'Up there,' said Wesson obscurely. 'Moss on the rock.'

'Paul, what?'

'We get changed,' said Wesson, stumbling out of the room again. 'We get changed. Like a piece of iron next to a magnet. Can't help it. You—nonmagnetic, I guess. Goes right through you, huh, Aunt Jane? You don't get changed. You stay here, wait for the next one.'

'. . . Yes,' said Aunt Jane.

'You know,' said Wesson, pacing, 'I can tell how he's lying up there. Head *that* way, tail the other. Am I right?'

'. . . Yes,' said Aunt Jane.

Wesson stopped, 'Yes,' he said intently. 'So you *can* tell me what you see up there, can't you, Aunt Jane?'

'No. Yes. It isn't allowed.'

'Listen, Aunt Jane, *we'll die* unless we can find out what makes those aliens tick! Remember that.' Wesson leaned against the corridor wall, gazing up. 'He's turning now—around this way. Right?

'Well, what else is he doing? Come on, Aunt Jane, tell me!'

A pause. 'He is twitching his——'

'What?'

'I don't know the words.'

'My God, my God,' said Wesson, clutching his head, 'of course there aren't any words.' He ran into the living room, clutched the console and stared at the blank screen. He pounded the metal with his fist. 'You've got to show me, Aunt Jane, come on and show me, show me!'

'It isn't allowed,' Aunt Jane protested.

'You've got to do it just the same, or we'll *die*, Aunt Jane—millions of us, billions, and it'll be your fault, get it, *your fault*, Aunt Jane!'

82

'*Please*,' said the voice. There was a pause. The screen flickered to life, for an instant only. Wesson had a glimpse of something massive and dark, but half transparent, like a magnified insect—a tangle of nameless limbs, whiplike filaments, claws, wings. . . .

He clutched at the edge of the console.

'Was that all right?' Aunt Jane asked.

'Of course! What do you think, it'll kill me to look at it? Put it back, Aunt Jane, put it back!'

Reluctantly, the screen lighted again. Wesson stared, and went on staring. He mumbled something.

'What?' said Aunt Jane.

'*Life of my love, I loathe thee*,' said Wesson, staring. He roused himself after a moment and turned away. The image of the alien stayed with him as he went reeling into the corridor again; he was not surprised to find that it reminded him of all the loathesome, crawling, creeping things the Earth was full of. That explained why he was not supposed to see the alien, or even know what it looked like—because that fed his hate. And it was all right for him to be afraid of the alien, but he was not supposed to hate it. . . . Why not? Why not?

His fingers were shaking. He felt drained, steamed, dried up and withered. The one daily shower Aunt Jane allowed him was no longer enough. Twenty minutes after bathing the acid sweat dripped again from his armpits, the cold sweat was beaded on his forehead, the hot sweat was in his palms. Wesson felt as if there were a furnace inside him, out of control, all the dampers drawn. He knew that under stress, something of the kind did happen to man: the body's chemistry was altered—more adrenalin, more glycogen in the muscles; eyes brighter, digestion retarded. That was the trouble—he was burning himself up, unable to fight the thing that tormented him, nor run from it.

After another circuit, Wesson's steps faltered. He hesitated, and went into the living room. He leaned over the console, staring. From the screen, the alien stared blindly up into space. Down in the dark side, the golden indicators had climbed: the vats were more than two-thirds filled.

. . . To *fight*, or *run*. . . .

Slowly Wesson sank down in front of the console. He sat hunched, head bent, hands squeezed tight between his knees, trying to hold onto the thought that had come to him.

If the alien felt a pain as great as Wesson's—or greater——

Stress might alter the alien's body chemistry, too.

Life of my love, I loathe thee.

Wesson pushed the irrelevant thought aside. He stared at the screen, trying to envisage the alien, up there, wincing in pain and distress—sweating a golden sweat of horror....

After a long time, he stood up and walked into the kitchen. He caught the table edge to keep his legs from carrying him on around the circuit. He sat down.

Humming fondly, the autochef slid out a tray of small glasses—water, orange juice, milk. Wesson put the water glass to his stiff lips; the water was cool and hurt his throat. Then the juice, but he could only drink a little of it; then he sipped the milk. Aunt Jane hummed approvingly.

Dehydrated—how long had it been since he had eaten, or drunk? He looked at his hands. They were thin bundles of sticks, ropy-veined, with hard yellow claws. He could see the bones of his forearms under the skin, and his heart's beating stirred the cloth at his chest. The pale hairs on his arms and thighs—were they blond or white?

The blurred reflections in the metal trim of the dining room gave him no answers—only pale faceless smears of gray. Wesson felt light-headed and very weak, as if he had just ended a bout of fever. He fumbled over his ribs and shoulder-bones. He was thin.

He sat in front of the autochef for a few minutes more, but no food came out. Evidently Aunt Jane did not think he was ready for it, and perhaps she was right. *Worse for them than for us,* he thought dizzily. *That's why the Station's so far out, why radio silence, and only one man aboard. They couldn't stand it all, otherwise....* Suddenly he could think of nothing but sleep—the bottomless pit, layer after layer of smothering velvet, numbing and soft.... His leg muscles quivered and twitched when he tried to walk, but he managed to get to the bedroom and fall on the mattress. The resilient block seemed to dissolve under him. His bones were melting.

He woke with a clear head, very weak, thinking cold and clear: *When two alien cultures meet, the stronger must transform the weaker with love or hate.* 'Wesson's Law,' he said aloud. He looked automatically for pencil and paper, but there was none, and he realised he would have to tell Aunt Jane, and let her remember it.

'I don't understand,' she said.

'Never mind, remember it anyway. You're good at that, aren't you?'

'Yes, Paul.'

'All right.... I want some breakfast.'

He thought about Aunt Jane, so nearly human, sitting up here in her metal prison, leading one man after another through the torment of hell ... nursemaid, protector, torturer. They must have known that something would have to give.... But the alphas were comparatively new; nobody understood them very well. Perhaps they really thought that an absolute prohibition could never be broken.

... the stronger must transform the weaker....

I'm *the stronger*, he thought. *And that's the way it's going to be.* He stopped at the console, and the screen was blank. He said angrily, 'Aunt Jane!' And with a guilty start, the screen flickered into life.

Up there, the alien had rolled again in his pain. Now the great clustered eyes were staring directly into the camera; the coiled limbs threshed in pain: the eyes were staring, asking, pleading....

'*No*,' said Wesson, feeling his own pain like an iron cap, and he slammed his hand down on the manual control. The screen went dark. He looked up, sweating, and saw the floral picture over the console.

The thick stems were like antennae, the leaves thoraxes, the buds like blind insect eyes. The whole picture moved slightly, endlessly, in a slow waiting rhythm.

Wesson clutched the hard metal of the console, and stared at the picture, with sweat cold on his brow, until it turned into a calm, meaningless arrangement of lines again. Then he went into the dining room, shaking, and sat down.

After a moment he said, 'Aunt Jane, does it get worse?'

'No. From now on, it gets better.'

'How long?' he asked vaguely.

'One month.'

A month, getting better ... that was the way it had always been, with the watchman swamped and drowned, his personality submerged. Wesson thought about the men who had gone before him—Class Seven citizenship, with unlimited leisure, and Class One housing, yes, sure—in a sanatorium.

His lips peeled back from his teeth, and his fists clenched hard. *Not me!* he thought.

He spread his hands on the cool metal to steady them. He said, 'How much longer do they usually stay able to talk?'

'You are already talking longer than any of them. . . .'

Then there was a blank. Wesson was vaguely aware, in snatches, of the corridor walls moving past, and the console glimpsed, and of a thunderous cloud of ideas that swirled around his head in a beating of wings. The aliens: what did they want? And what happened to the watchmen in Stranger Station?

The haze receded a little and he was in the dining room again, staring vacantly at the table. Something was wrong.

He ate a few spoonsful of the gruel the autochef served him, then pushed it away; the stuff tasted faintly unpleasant. The machine hummed anxiously and thrust a poached egg at him, but Wesson got up from the table.

The Station was all but silent. The resting rhythm of the household machines throbbed in the walls, unheard. The blue-lit living room was spread out before him like an empty stage setting, and Wesson stared as if he had never seen it before.

He lurched to the console and stared down at the pictured alien on the screen: heavy, heavy, a-sprawl with pain in the darkness. The needles of the golden indicators were high, the enlarged vats almost full. *It's too much for him*, Wesson thought with grim satisfaction. The peace that followed the pain had not descended as it was supposed to; no, not this time!

He glanced up at the painting over the console: heavy crustacean limbs that swayed gracefully in the sea. . . .

He shook his head violently. *I won't let it; I won't give in!*

He held the back of one hand close to his eyes. He saw the dozens of tiny cuneiform wrinkles stamped into the skin over the knuckles, the pale hairs sprouting, the pink shiny flesh of recent scars. *I'm human*, he thought. But when he let his hand fall onto the console, the bony fingers seemed to crouch like crustaceans' legs, ready to scuttle.

Sweating, Wesson stared into the screen. Pictured there, the alien met his eyes, and it was as if they spoke to each other, mind to mind, an instantaneous communication that needed no words. There was a piercing sweetness to it, a melting, dissolving luxury of change into something that would no longer have any pain. . . . A pull, a calling.

Wesson straightened up slowly, carefully, as if he held some fragile thing in his mind that must not be handled roughly, or it would disintegrate. He said hoarsely, 'Aunt Jane!'

She made some responsive noise.

He said, 'Aunt Jane, I've got the answer! The whole thing! Listen, now wait—listen!' He paused a moment to collect his thoughts. *'When two alien cultures meet, the stronger must transform the weaker with love or hate.* Remember? You said you didn't understand what that meant. I'll *tell* you what it means. When these—monsters—met Pigeon a hundred years ago on Titan, *they knew* we'd have to meet again. They're spreading out, colonising, and so are we. We haven't got interstellar flight yet, but give us another hundred years, we'll *get* it. *We'll wind up out there, where they are.* And they can't stop us. Because they're not killers, Aunt Jane, it isn't in them. They're *nicer* than us. See, they're like the missionaries, and we're the South Sea Islanders. *They* don't kill their enemies, oh no—perish the thought!'

She was trying to say something, to interrupt him, but he rushed on. 'Listen! The longevity serum—that was a lucky accident. But they played it for all it's worth. Slick and smooth—they come and give us the stuff free—they don't ask for a thing in return. Why not? Listen.

'They come here, and the shock of that first contact makes them sweat out that golden gook we need. Then, the last month or so, the pain always eases off. Why? Because the two minds, the human and alien, they stop fighting each other.

87

Something gives way, it goes soft, and there's a mixing together. And that's where you get the human casualties of this operation—the bleary men that come out of here not even able to talk human language any more. Oh, I suppose they're happy—happier than I am!—because they've got something big and wonderful inside 'em. Something that you and I can't even understand. But if you took them and put them together again with the aliens who spent time here, *they could all live together—they're adapted*.

'That's what they're aiming for!' He struck the console with his fist. 'Not now—but a hundred, two hundred years from now! When we start expanding out to the stars—when we go a-conquering—we'll have already been conquered! Not by weapons, Aunt Jane, not by hate—by love! Yes, love! *Dirty, stinking, low-down, sneaking love!*'

Aunt Jane said something, a long sentence, in a high, anxious voice.

'What?' said Wesson irritably. He couldn't understand a word.

Aunt Jane was silent. 'What, what?' Wesson demanded, pounding the console. 'Have you got it through your tin head or not? *What?*'

Aunt Jane said something else, tonelessly. Once more, Wesson could not make out a single word.

He stood frozen. Warm tears started suddenly out of his eyes. 'Aunt Jane——' he said. He remembered, *You are already talking longer than any of them.* Too late? Too late? He tensed, then whirled and sprang to the closet where the paper books were kept. He opened the first one his hand struck.

The black letters were alien squiggles on the page, little humped shapes, without meaning.

The tears were coming faster, he couldn't stop them: tears of weariness, tears of frustration, tears of hate. '*Aunt Jane!*' he roared.

But it was no good. The curtain of silence had come down over his head. He was one of the vanguard—the conquered men, the ones who would get along with their strange brothers, out among the alien stars.

The console was not working any more; nothing worked when he wanted it. Wesson squatted in the shower stall, naked, with a soup bowl in his hands. Water droplets glistened on his hands and forearms; the pale short hairs were just springing up, drying.

The silvery skin of reflection in the bowl gave him back nothing but a silhouette, a shadow man's outline. He could not see his face.

He dropped the bowl and went across the living room, shuffling the pale drifts of paper underfoot. The black lines on the paper, when his eye happened to light on them, were worm shapes, crawling things, conveying nothing. He rolled slightly in his walk; his eyes were glazed. His head twitched, every now and then, sketching a useless motion to avoid pain.

Once the bureau chief, Gower, came to stand in his way. 'You fool,' he said, his face contorted in anger, 'you were supposed to go on to the end, like the rest. Now look what you've done!'

'I found out, didn't I?' Wesson mumbled, and as he brushed the man aside like a cobweb, the pain suddenly grew more intense. Wesson clasped his head in his hands with a grunt, and rocked to and fro a moment, uselessly, before he straightened and went on. The pain was coming in waves now, so tall that at their peak his vision dimmed out, violet, then gray.

It couldn't go on much longer. Something had to burst.

He paused at the bloody place and slapped the metal with his palm, making the sound ring dully up into the frame of the Station: *rroom, rroom.*

Faintly an echo came back: boo-oom.

Wesson kept going, smiling a faint and meaningless smile. He was only marking time now, waiting. Something was about to happen.

The kitchen doorway sprouted a sudden sill and tripped him. He fell heavily, sliding on the floor, and lay without moving beneath the slick gleam of the autochef.

The pressure was too great: the autochef's clucking was swallowed up in the ringing pressure, and the tall gray walls buckled slowly in. . . .

The Station lurched.

Wesson felt it through his chest, palms, knees and elbows: the floor was plucked away for an instant and then swung back.

The pain in his skull relaxed its grip a little. Wesson tried to get to his feet.

There was an electric silence in the Station. On the second try, he got up and leaned his back against a wall. *Cluck*, said the autochef suddenly, hysterically, and the vent popped open, but nothing came out.

He listened, straining to hear. What?

The Station bounced beneath him, making his feet jump like a puppet's; the wall slapped his back hard, shuddered and was still; but far off through the metal cage came a long angry groan of metal, echoing, diminishing, dying. Then silence again.

The Station held its breath. All the myriad clickings and pulses in the walls were suspended; in the empty rooms the lights burned with a yellow glare, and the air hung stagnant and still. The console lights in the living room glowed like witchfires. Water on the dropped bowl, at the bottom of the shower stall, shone like quicksilver, waiting.

The third shock came. Wesson found himself on his hands and knees, the jolt still tingling in the bones of his body, staring at the floor. The sound that filled the room ebbed away slowly and ran down into the silences: a resonant metallic sound, shuddering away now along the girders and hull plates, rattling tinnily into bolts and fittings, diminishing, noiseless, gone. The silence pressed down again.

The floor leaped painfully under his body: one great resonant blow that shook him from head to foot.

A muted echo of that blow came a few seconds later, as if the shock had traveled across the Station and back.

The bed, Wesson thought, and scrambled on hands and knees through the doorway, along a floor curiously tilted, until he reached the rubbery block.

The room burst visibly upward around him, squeezing the block flat. It dropped back as violently, leaving Wesson bouncing helplessly on the mattress, his limbs flying. It came to rest, in a long reluctant groan of metal.

Wesson rolled up on one elbow, thinking incoherently, *Air, the air lock.* Another blow slammed him down into the mattress, pinched his lungs shut, while the room danced grotesquely over his head. Gasping for breath in the ringing silence, Wesson felt a slow icy chill rolling toward him across the room ... and there was a pungent smell in the air. *Ammonia!* he thought; and the odorless, smothering methane with it.

His cell was breached. The burst membrane was fatal: the alien's atmosphere would kill him.

Wesson surged to his feet. The next shock caught him off balance, dashed him to the floor. He arose again, dazed and limping; he was still thinking confusedly, *The air lock, get out.*

When he was halfway to the door, all the ceiling lights went out at once. The darkness was like a blanket around his head. It was bitter cold now in the room and the pungent smell was sharper. Coughing, Wesson hurried forward. The floor lurched under his feet.

Only the golden indicators burned now: full to the top, the deep vats brimming, golden-lipped, gravid, a month before the time. Wesson shuddered.

Water spurted in the bathroom, hissing steadily on the tiles, rattling in the plastic bowl at the bottom of the shower stall. The lights winked on and off again. In the dining room, he heard the autochef clucking and sighing. The freezing wind blew harder: he was numb with cold to the hips. It seemed to Wesson abruptly that he was not at the top of the sky at all, but down, *down* at the bottom of the sea ... trapped in this steel bubble, while the dark poured in.

The pain in his head was gone, as if it had never been there, and he understood what that meant: Up there, the great body was hanging like a butcher's carrion in the darkness. Its death struggles were over, the damage done.

Wesson gathered a desperate breath, shouted, 'Help me! The alien's dead! He kicked the Station apart—the methane's coming in! Get help, do you hear me? *Do you hear me?*'

Silence. In the smothering blackness, he remembered: *She can't understand me any more. Even if she's alive.*

He turned, making an animal noise in his throat. He groped his way on around the room, past the second doorway. Behind the walls, something was dripping with a slow cold tinkle and splash, a forlorn night sound. Small, hard, floating things rapped against his legs. Then he touched a smooth curve of metal: the airlock.

Eagerly he pushed his feeble weight against the door. It didn't move. Cold air was rushing out around the door frame, a thin knife-cold stream, but the door itself was jammed tight.

The suit! He should have thought of that before. If he just had some pure air to breathe, and a little warmth in his fingers. ... But the door of the suit locker would not move, either. The ceiling must have buckled.

And that was the end, he thought, bewildered. There were no more ways out. But there *had* to be—— He pounded on the door until his arms would not lift any more; it did not move. Leaning against the chill metal, he saw a single light blink on overhead.

The room was a wild place of black shadows and swimming shapes—the book leaves, fluttering and darting in the air stream. Schools of them beat wildly at the walls, curling over, baffled, trying again; others were swooping around the outer corridor, around and around: he could see them whirling past the doorways, dreamlike, a white drift of silent paper in the darkness.

The acrid smell was harsher to his nostrils. Wesson choked, groping his way to the console again. He pounded it with his open hand, crying weakly: he wanted to see Earth.

But when the little square of brightness leaped up, it was the dead body of the alien that Wesson saw.

It hung motionless in the cavity of the Station, limbs dangling stiff and still, eyes dull. The last turn of the screw had been too much for it: but Wesson had survived. ...

For a few minutes.

The dead alien face mocked him; a whisper of memory floated into his mind: *We might have been brothers.* ... All at once Wesson passionately wanted to believe it—wanted to give in, turn back. That passed. Wearily he let himself sag into the bitter *now*, thinking with thin defiance, *It's done—hate wins. You'll have to stop this big giveaway—can't risk this happening again. And we'll hate you for that—and when we get out to the stars——*

The world was swimming numbly away out of reach. He felt the last fit of coughing take his body, as if it were happening to someone else besides him.

The last fluttering leaves of paper came to rest. There was a long silence in the drowned room.

Then:

'Paul,' said the voice of the mechanical woman brokenly; 'Paul,' it said again, with the hopelessness of lost, unknown, impossible love.

IT began with the crutch. Then came the iron hook, then the first mechanical limbs. And finally——

Bedlam. Thin metal legs switching by, a moving forest of scissors. Metal arms flashing in balance; torsos of metal, like bright dented beetles. Round metal skulls—that cupped the swift wink and stare of human eyes.

Krisch, watching them in his desk scanner, kept the volume turned down. The unit walls were deliberately made sound-reflecting; the children grew up in the atmosphere of their own clattering noise, and they learned to shout against it. To soldiers so reared, there would be no terror in the roar of battle. But Krisch, who was only human, wore earplugs when he walked among them.

The river of metal funneled into classrooms, stopped. Lights flashed on over the scanners, on the board that covered the twenty-foot wall facing Krisch's desk. Instruction had begun.

Krisch watched the board for a while, then switched on the illuminated panel that carried his notes and began to dictate his weekly report. He was a small, spare man, with thinning strands of iron-gray hair roached stiffly back over his freckled brown scalp. His mouth was straight, and the lines around it showed that he never smiled; but there was a glint of controlled, ironic humor in his watchful eyes.

A bell spoke and a red light gleamed. Krisch looked up sharply, identified the scanner under the warning light, and transferred its image to his own desk screen. Half a thousand pairs of eyes stared back at him from the massed metal forms in the amphitheater.

Krisch set the playback cube for one minute preceding. The robot instructors were equipped to answer all permissible questions; therefore a nonpermissible question had just been asked.

The harsh voice of the robot said, '—along the inguinal canal and enters the abdomen through the internal abdominal ring. Yes? What is your question?'

There was a pause. Krisch scanned the rows of gleaming heads, could not tell which one had signaled 'Question.' Then the abnormally loud but still childish voice spoke, and simultaneously the student's number appeared in the recording circle at the lower left corner of the screen. Krisch statted it automatically. The ten-year-old voice bellowed:

'What is a kiss?'

There was a five-second pause. The robot answered, 'Your question is meaningless. It has been reported to the Director and you will hold yourself in readiness for his orders.' Then it resumed its lecture.

Krisch switched the scanner back to normal operation. The robot was now discussing the prostate gland. Krisch waited until it had reached the end of a sentence and then pressed the 'Attention' button on his console. He said, 'Cadet ER17235 will report to the Director's office immediately.' He cleared the board and sank into his cushioned chair, frowning.

A nonpermissible question was bad enough in itself; there had not been one in the oldest class in the last six years of the Project's existence. It was not only bad; it was indefensible. Logically, it should not have happened—the entire student body of the unit, according to a check made not a week ago, was correctly conditioned.

But that was not all. The robot instructor had been perfectly truthful, to the extent of its own knowledge, when it had said the cadet's question was meaningless. The subject of normal human love relationships was not on the curriculum for two more years. To introduce it earlier, with the desired effect of repugnance, would seriously damage discipline.

Krisch turned his selector to the appropriate list, but he knew the answer already. The word 'kiss' was not in the student's vocabulary. And there was no one in the Unit, besides himself, from whom the cadet could have learned it.

Krisch stood up and went to the transparent wall behind his

desk—one huge window that looked out on the parade ground and beyond it to the chill, airless surface of the planet. Only starlight gleamed from the jagged points of that landscape which faced eternally away from the sun; the force screen that maintained the Unit's atmosphere also acted as a light trap. Krisch could look up and see, one thousand light years away, the cold dim glow that was the cluster of which Cynara was a part, and the whole frightening majesty of space in between. But a hypothetical enemy scout, pausing in space to scan this waste planet, would see nothing but tiny disk of blackness that might be a vitreous plain, or the crater of a long-dead volcano.

Krisch had been here a little more than ten years, moving along from one installation to the next with his class, turning over the vacated office and its duties to the next lowest man in the hierarchy. Each year a new Director was shipped out with a new load of embryos and equipment, and at the end of ten more years Krisch would be permanently installed as Director of the final Unit, and as senior officer of the entire Project. That was all he had to look forward to, for the rest of his life. Many ships arrived here, but none left, or would ever leave, except those that carried the troops themselves when they were needed. Krisch's rewards were solitude, achievement, power, and the partial satisfaction of boundless curiosity.

His penalty, if the Project were to fail or even be seriously delayed while it was under his command, would be painful in the extreme.

The door speaker said, 'Cadet ER17235 reporting as ordered, sir.'

Krisch returned to his desk. He said, 'Enter.'

The metal thing stalked into the room and stood at attention in front of the Director's desk. Only the irreducible minimum of it was organic: the boy's head, pared to a functional ball, the blue eyes staring through the metal skull piece, a surgically simplified torso, the limb stumps. By itself it would be no more than a disgusting, useless lump of meat; but, housed in the metal body, it was a sketch of the perfect fighting man.

The cadet, like the rest of his class, was only ten years old;

the living part of him had been transferred many times from one articulated metal shell to another. For that reason his present body was comparatively crude. When he had reached his full growth he would be given his final body—so fantastically armored as to be almost indestructible, so powerful that it could outrun any land vehicle over broken terrain. The weapons built into his arms, controlled directly by his nerves, would be sufficient to destroy a city. And he would be completely without fear.

Krisch let the silence frown between them while the boy stood at attention. Just now the boy knew fear. It was necessary for discipline, and the repressed hostility toward Krisch would later be translated into a useful hatred for all non-mechanical human beings. To use physical pain as a means of punishment was out of the question. That, in fact, was the root idea of the entire Project.

The crutch went back to prehistoric times. The metal hook, to replace a lost hand, was born early in the Iron Age. The Twentieth Century knew prosthetic devices which looked almost like flesh, and adequately performed all mechanical functions of natural limbs. But it remained for the galactic culture and the warlike nation which Krisch was a part of to discover that artificial limbs could be more than a lesser evil; that the metal arm, the metal finger, was better than flesh. Better. Its cleverly articulated segments reported pressure, temperature and position as well as flesh. Its strength was incomparably greater. And it felt no pain.

Man is so soft, thought Krisch, in comparison with the metal he uses; so soft, and so easily hurt. Every cubic inch of flesh, excepting only the brain itself, contains its minuscule fuse of agony. But metal feels no pain. Those boys will conquer the galaxy; no human troops can stand against them.

He amended the thought. Five minutes ago that had been almost a certainty. Now, it was only possible.

He said, 'Where did you learn the word "kiss"?'

The boy's eyelids fluttered behind the steel mask. 'From a——' He hesitated. 'A training device, sir,' he finished uncertainly.

Krisch said sharply, 'Are you sure?'

97

A long pause. 'I—I think it was, sir.'

'You *think* it was,' said Krisch. 'Describe this "training device."'

'It's—like a human being, sir.'

'Mechanised, or all flesh?'

Silence. The boy's eyelids blinked, and Krisch could imagine the rest of the face, screwed up in an agony of uncertainty. 'Answer the question,' he said.

'Neither one, sir,' said the boy painfully. 'It was——'

'Well? What was it made of?'

'Of——'

'Well?'

'Of—just lines, sir.'

Krisch sat back a moment, looking at the cadet in frowning silence. The boy's hesitant answers showed either that he was lying—which was inconceivable—or that he was conscious of guilt.

'Of just lines,' he repeated. He put a skeptical note into his voice. 'Explain.'

'That's all, sir,' the boy said eagerly. 'It was made of lines, and it looked like a human being, and it talked to me.' His voice stopped abruptly.

Krisch pounced on that. 'What did it talk about?'

'About—about love, sir.'

Another word the cadets had not been taught. 'Go on,' said Krisch. 'What did it say about love?'

'About human beings meeting, flesh to flesh, and—how good it was. About one human being loving another one—it said that means when you know the other human being is lonely and afraid like you, and you give the other one part of the way you feel about yourself, instead of keeping it all. And you show how you feel by meeting flesh to flesh, and it makes you feel wonderful, like killing something, but much better.' The cadet paused. 'But I didn't understand about kisses. It seemed to be very complicated.'

Krisch felt a ball of coldness settle in his chest. This boy was ruined; he would have to be scrapped. And how many others?

'Where did all this take place?' he demanded.

'During airless maneuvers yesterday, sir.'

Krisch tried to visualise it: the cadets scattered out there in the cold blackness, carrying out one of the prescribed war games under the direction of student squad leaders. One of them isolated from the rest, waiting for a signal. And while he waited—something—had approached him, and spoken to him of love. . . .

'No one else saw or heard?'

'No, sir.'

'Why did you fail to report it?'

A pause. 'I—I thought it was part of the training.'

'Tell the truth!' Krisch snapped.

The cadet's eyes blinked. As Krisch watched, horrified, they grew unmistakably moist. 'I—don't know, sir! I don't know!'

The moisture brimmed over: two tears ran down the shining mask that was the boy's face.

Another signal light blinked red on the master board. Then another. Krisch knew, finally, that the test had come ten years ahead of time: the Project was at war.

Krisch strapped himself into the speedster and eased it out through the exit tunnel. He had put the entire student body through interrogation and a psych check, and had turned up fifty-three more cases of induced aberration. For the time being he had left them all at liberty but carefully monitored; he hoped that one of them might be approached again by the saboteur, whoever or whatever it was.

Something flashed dully in the starlight outside the transparent nose of the speedster. Krisch stared at it, then inched the speedster over until the object lay almost directly under him.

It was a cadet, without the space gear that should have closed the openings in his faceplate and made his body airtight. The body was sprawled lifelessly. The staring eyes were blood red with burst capillaries.

Krisch peered through the transparent metal and read the serial number etched into the cadet's foreskull. It was the boy he had interviewed an hour ago.

He contacted his desk relays and gave orders for the disposal of the body and the detention of the other fifty-three. For the moment, it was all he could do.

He took the speedster up and set its course toward Unit 1, three hundred miles away. After his interview with Cadet ER17235, he had called the Directors of the other nine installations and ordered immediate psych checks. The results, gathered two hours later, showed that every unit had been affected. Viar, Director of Unit 1 and the newest member of the Project's staff, had had an additional and equally disturbing report to make.

Krisch watched the backdrop of white fire and black velvet move ponderously past. Even if he were able to remove the disturbing factor before it had done further harm, it might prove impossible to knit the structure together again. The oldest of the cadets had not yet reached the stage in which the circle of their conditioning would be unbreakable. Normal emotions and a normal biological life had no place in that circle; but it was still possible to introduce them. The result was—insanity. A flood of emotion for which no outlet had been or could be provided; impossible desires: the classic insoluble dilemma.

He remembered the blood-red, staring eyes of the dead boy. The symbolism was appropriate. His eyes were the only organs of expression left to him; and he had certainly used them effectively enough.

For the first time in many years, the Director wished he had not been born into a nation with a history of thwarted development and a psychology of resentment. He wished that he were an underpaid pedagogue on a world at peace. He wished that he had not been forced by circumstances to put that boy in a metal cage.

Viar met him, by request, at the bottom level of Unit 1—the level that housed the huge atomic converter which powered the unit. Viar was a youngish man with a large, white, perspiring face that expressed conscientiousness and insecurity. His eyes were milk-blue, surrounded by white lashes. Krisch disliked him thoroughly.

They stood by the shaft that the converter had dug in the stone of the planet. Viar said nervously, 'I first noticed that we had stumbled on something when I checked the meter readings. They showed mostly granite, but there were occasional fluctuations that indicated refined metal. I was curious, so I set the converter to extract only the stone. Yesterday I shut off the converter briefly, and sent a cadet down to see what was left.'

Krisch looked at the curious array of objects spread out on the plastic floor. There were three metal tablets incised with neat rows of dots, ovals, squares, and crosses. There was a long curved trough, with an attachment at one end that suggested it might have been designed to fit a wrist—or a tentacle. There was a set of concentric ellipses, with little balls that seemed designed to run along them; clearly an orrery of this solar system. There was a six-foot metal box, curiously fashioned in a complexity of intersecting planes.

Krisch knew that this world could not have supported indigenous life more recently than ten million years ago; but there was not a trace of corrosion in any of the artifacts.

He said, 'Why did you fail to report this until I called you?'

Viar said apologetically, 'I thought it could wait for my weekly report. It didn't seem to have any importance, until today. Then I noticed that this box was open.'

Krisch looked at it. The seam gaped very slightly around three sides. He tested it, and found that the enclosed face would not move in either direction. It seemed unlikely that anything but a gas could have escaped.

He remembered the dead cadet's description of the strange thing that had spoken to him on the training ground. 'It was made of lines. . . .' None of the others had duplicated this phrase: they had simply said that it was like a man, but different. The fanciful thought occurred to him that if the first description was correct, and the word 'lines' had been used mathematically, even this millimeter gap would not have been necessary.

'Is it possible that one of the cadets could have opened it?' he demanded.

'Perhaps,' Viar granted, willing to consider every possibility, 'but it does not seem probable.' He gestured toward the box. 'I made several attempts to open it when I first got it out,' he said. 'Perhaps something I did had a delayed action. At any rate, I would swear that not only was it heavier then than it is now, but there was a force lock of some nature holding it shut. I've looked in with a microprobe, and there is a small mechanism of some kind attached to one corner. I believe the box can be opened fully now, but I thought I had better wait until you could inspect it.'

'You believe, then,' said Krisch, 'that there was a device in this thing which was still in operation until yesterday?'

Viar looked at him with a trace of hangdog defiance. 'I believe that there was something in that box which is still operating, *now.*'

Krisch controlled his irritation and said nothing. Viar escorted him back to the exit tube. Krisch told him, 'Proceed with normal activities, but monitor every cadet. And open that box, but not inside the Unit. And report to me hourly.' He strapped himself into the speedster again and turned its nose back to Unit Ten.

Three more cases of aberrant conduct were waiting for him, and the reports from the other units were similar and equally alarming. Krisch interviewed a few more, then cubed a standard interview form and turned the process over to robot mechanisms. Viar called him later in the day, to report that he had succeeded in opening the box but could make nothing of its contents.

Krisch got the collated reports from the robot interviewers and ran up a tentative prediction. In twenty-six hours the unknown agent—which might or might not have escaped from the box unearthed by Viar—had corrupted one hundred and fifty-three cadets, or approximately one every ten minutes. If it continued at the same rate, which of course could not be assumed with so little data, ten per cent of the total student body would have been aberrated at the end of three hundred hours. Twelve and a half Galactic Standard days—and at the end of that time, Krisch reckoned grimly, the Project would be hopelessly crippled.

Monitoring the cadets had been totally ineffective; Krisch ordered it discontinued. His only other defensive move would have been to suspend normal activities altogether and keep the cadets in monitored groups, but that would have had a psychological effect nearly as bad as the one he was trying to avert. He ordered the aberrees to be confined and then destroyed personally by the Director of each Unit, without the knowledge of the student leaders.

He carried out this duty himself in Unit Ten, and then went to bed.

He awoke from a nightmare in which he had been surrounded by silent metal bodies—the bodies of ten-year-old cadets; but instead of the egg-shaped headpieces, they had worn open helmets; and where their faces should have been were raw, bleeding disks of flesh.

Deliberately he relaxed his body and sank back onto the sweat-drenched cushion. Then he sat up again with a start, realising that what had waked him had been someone's entrance into the room.

And that was simply, starkly impossible. His apartment was guarded while he slept by armored walls and a massive door which would have held back a regiment. Moreover, there were alarm devices which would signal any attempt to enter. Still further, no one in this Unit or any other had the slightest sane motive for trying to enter without permission.

That realisation exploded in his mind, and faded against the fact registered by the outmost corner of his vision: there was someone in the room.

He raised his head, looking full at the archway that separated his sleeping room from his office. There was a dim glow from the instrument panels.

A strange man stood there.

That was his first dominant impression; and it was so strong that for a long minute, even while he saw that he was mistaken, he could not rid himself of it.

The eye does not see a man; it sees a grouping of lines which are capable of almost infinite variation. The visual center interprets those lines, compares them with a *gestalt*, a perception-of-form, and the mind says, 'Man.'

With an effort, Krisch put aside his preconceptions and accepted what he saw.

He saw a collection of lines that enclosed no form. The glow from his office shone between them. There was a series of curlicues that might have suggested hair; then a gap; then two incomplete spirals that vaguely suggested eyes; another gap; and a straight line for a nose; farther down, a line for the mouth, curved into an idiotic smile. On either side was a handle-shaped line for the ear.

The body was like that of a stick man drawn by a child; one line for the torso, two for the arms, two for the legs, and three stiffly curling lines for each hand.

The figure said, 'Ask me anything.'

The voice spoke without sound, the words coming spontaneously into Krisch's mind as if written with a phosphorescent crayon on a sheet of black glass. Krisch realised this without surprise, and briefly wondered why: then he recalled the interview with the first cadet. The boy had said he had spoken with the 'training device' outside the Unit area, during airless maneuvers.

Krisch thought, 'Who are you?'

The answer was immediate. 'I am a device to entertain and instruct you. Ask me anything.'

Krisch's hand rested on the button that controlled a battery of force pencils focused on the area in front of his couch, but he had no intention of using it. There was every reason to suspect that such methods would fail; and if they did he would have surrendered his only chance.

He decided to take the thing at its word. 'How can you be destroyed?'

'I can not be destroyed.'

'How can you be immobilised, then?'

'By——' The figure went without a pause, but the visual images replaced the words. There were, Krisch realised, no words in his language for those images. They flashed briefly before him, each one trailing glimpses of the process that produced it. Krisch could not even retain the sequence, much less interpret it. 'Repeat,' he thought.

The same images came and went; and at the end of it, Krisch knew that he would never learn anything useful from them. What he was seeing was the terminal end of a thousand-year chain of technology. He could not expect to grasp it from one simple explanation, any more than a savage could be taught metallurgy in a sentence.

Krisch remembered, with panic, that the thing's average indoctrination period was ten minutes. He said, 'What governs the length of time you stay with one person?'

'If he asks me to stay, I stay.'

Krisch relaxed for the first time since he had seen the figure standing there in the doorway. If that were true then his battle was won. 'There are a great many questions I want to ask you,' he thought. 'Stay with me until I ask you to go.'

There was no reply. He demanded, 'Will you do as I ask?'

'Yes.'

Fully awake now, Krisch raised the backrest of the cushion and pressed the buttons for nourishment. His mind was racing. A thought was half born in his mind that made him tremble. He asked, 'Of what substance are you composed?'

The figure said, 'Of no substance. I am the Pattern.'

Krisch leaned forward. 'Do you mean that you are not material?' he demanded.

'I am not material. I am a pattern of forces which adapts itself to each individual I serve. You see the sketch of a man; my makers would see something quite different.'

'Are you intelligent?'

'I am not intelligent. I have no will or independent existence. I am merely a device for answering questions.'

Krisch thought for a moment. He said, 'A minute ago you described yourself as *the* Pattern. Does that mean you are the only one of your kind ever created?'

'No. There were many others, but those who came after my makers did not like us. We disturbed them. Therefore they imprisoned us, like the jinn in your legend, since they could not destroy us.'

Krisch asked, 'Are you capable of lying?'

'No.'

That was the central question, and unfortunately the answer meant nothing. But Krisch was beginning to see a strong possibility that his first estimate of the thing as a saboteur was mistaken. The other explanation fitted the facts more readily and completely. The Pattern was what it called itself, 'a device to entertain and instruct you.' It presented itself to a cadet who was alone and idle—probably it had been designed never to interfere with anyone who had something better to do. The cadet asked questions; the Pattern answered them. At the end of ten minutes or so—a cadet was rarely unoccupied for longer —the cadet released it and it looked for another client.

And because the fields about which the cadets were most curious were precisely those whose knowledge would destroy them—they went insane.

The Pattern had said that 'those who came after my makers did not like us.' It was understandable. Every culture had its areas of forbidden knowledge and politely ignored facts. The Pattern would be inhibited in those areas—where its own makers were concerned. But in an alien society, its truthful answers could be explosive.

He asked, 'Were you intended for the use of children, or of adults?'

'For the use of both.'

The knowledge he wanted was there, then, and by asking enough questions, he could get it. You could not teach metallurgy to a savage in one sentence, or even in one day—but you could teach him.

Assuming that the pattern was truthful, there was still one open question that gave Krisch reason to hesitate. An absolutely truthful oracle could be a dangerous thing: witness the insanity of the cadets, and the 'disturbance' of 'those who came after our makers.' Krisch's mind was not the artificial, delicately balanced creation that the cadets' were, but he knew very well that he had areas of instability; he could even concede that there might be such areas of which he was not aware. Could he ask the right questions—the ones which would not evoke dangerous answers?

He thought so. What he wanted from the pattern was nothing that could be intimately bound up with his emotional drives or the structure of his ego; he wanted technical information.

Prove to a religious fanatic that there is no God, and you

destroy him. But give him a flame thrower, and he will destroy the ungodly.

Finally, there was the question that capped all others: just how had the Pattern kept up an average rate of one cadet every ten minutes—counting the time spent in traveling from one Unit to the next, and in finding an available subject?

The answer was the one he had suspected and hoped for: the Pattern moved by instantaneous transport, out of the normal fabric of spacetime.

'How?' asked Krisch. Again he got a series of incomprehensible images. 'Explain that first picture,' said Krisch, and, 'Break that down further,' and 'What is that component?' And, very slowly, the Pattern began to teach him.

The problem of limiting the Pattern's activities while Krisch slept bothered him. He solved it, finally, by setting up a pool of cadets to be admitted by a robot monitor, one at a time, into a room where the Pattern could talk to them without interruption. As soon as one cadet stopped asking questions, he was removed and another was admitted. Krisch found that although the Pattern could plant the seeds of insanity in a cadet in less than ten minutes, it took an average of nearly two hours to reduce the same cadet to such a mindless state that he was no longer useful as a questioner. Thus, during each of Krisch's six-hour sleep periods, the Pattern disposed of only three cadets. During the remaining eighteen hours of each day, Krisch kept it fully occupied.

All knowledge is power, rightfully applied. But Krisch needed a particular kind of lever and a special place to stand. Slowly and painfully he was getting it.

The balance of forces which had made the cadets possible and necessary included, as one of its basic assumptions, transport at finite speeds. Under this limiting condition, attack from space on a fortified planet was enormously costly and by itself could not succeed. It was necessary for the attacker to expend twenty ships in order to land one: thereafter the war proceeded on the ground, under the enemy's own defensive umbrella, as wars had always been fought—in hand-to-hand, street-to-street combat. Superiority in ground troops, therefore could be the decisive factor.

But an object moving instantaneously could not, by definition, be interrupted or affected in any way while in transit. And therefore: the man who brought the secret of such transport to Cynara or any other great power could ask his own price. Since the power which brought the secret would shortly rule the galaxy, the price would be high.

If Krisch had been required to understand everything he was taught, the project would have been nearly hopeless. As it was, his task was difficult enough. The Pattern's knowledge included minutely detailed plans for every stage of the operation that were required, and for all the subsidiary operations that produced the components, and the still more subsidiary operations that produced *them*. Krisch had to follow these step by painful step, like a savage smelting ore to build a smeltery to smelt the ore better, to build a foundry to cast the metal to make tools that made other tools that built a machine that built another machine to draw wire, that another machine shaped and threaded: result, a bolt.

He stopped sending his weekly reports. The next ship to Cynara was not due for six months, and it would take more than two years for a ship to reach him after his message carriers stopped arriving. He glanced at the master board in his office only twice a day, when he awoke and before he went to bed; the rest of the time he spent with the Pattern in the Unit's machine shops and laboratories. Minor breakdowns occurred, but he grudged the time to attend to them. Repair machines broke down and were not replaced from stock: thereafter, when anything went wrong with a robot instructor or monitor, it remained out of action. Cadets went to their assigned classrooms but heard no lectures. Krisch saw a few of these, with more initiative than the rest, wandering around the corridors. He ignored them. The Project simply did not matter any longer, by comparison with the weapon he was forging under the Pattern's direction.

He allowed the weekly cubes from the other nine Directors to pile up unread on his desk. On the fifteenth morning the green light of the inter-unit communicator was blinking as he entered his office. He clicked over the switch and saw Viar's

108

round, perspiring face on the screen. Viar said: 'Director Krisch! I've been trying to get you since eighteen hours yesterday. Is anything wrong at your Unit?'

'Nothing's wrong,' said Krisch curtly. 'I've been very busy. What is it you want?'

'Why, I was only wondering if you'd decided what action to take on the special report I sent you last week. I don't want to press you, but——'

'I'm considering it,' Krisch said. 'I'll let you know as soon as I reach a decision. Is there anything else?'

'Just one other thing—I was wondering if there had been any more trouble with the saboteur in your Unit. I haven't had any for two weeks, now, and——'

'Nor I,' said Krisch. 'There's nothing we can do on that score until it appears again, if it does.'

He broke the contact and sorted the message cubes on his desk until he found the one labeled 'Unit 1—1/17/09— Special.' He dropped it into the viewer and scanned it quickly. It appeared that Viar had been doing more archeological research on his own initiative. Krisch repressed a stab of irritation and read on. Viar had widened the converter's field and increased its output, using the surplus to turn out ingots for small converter units, in order to excavate a pit two hundred feet square by one hundred feet deep. The objects he had so far extracted showed clearly, he said, that two entirely distinct cultures were represented. Those that Krisch had already seen, including the enigmatic box, belonged to the later culture, and these included several artifacts which Viar considered to be weapons. Krisch frowned over this section; it was not elaborated.

Viar's main point was that, judging, by pictograms and items shaped to the wearers' use, the first culture had been so alien biologically and sociologically as to be almost incomprehensible—but the latecomers had been men. Viar suggested, with a breathless tone showing through his careful phrases, that this was a discovery of enormous importance to galactic archeology and anthropology. Radioactive tests confirmed their previous estimate that the planet had been dead for more than ten million years. Therefore the conclusion was inescapable that mankind had not originated on Earth or Sol—that there had been a previous wave of colonisation, so ancient that no trace of it had ever been found before.

Viar, Krisch thought contemptuously, envisioned a future of academic glory. He wanted Krisch to authorise him to dispatch his finds immediately to Cynara, with the recommendation that a research group be set up on the Project planet—to be headed, no doubt, by Viar himself.

The notion of independent evolution did not even seem to have occurred to him.

The obvious thing to do was to keep him contented, and Krisch was inclined to doubt that Viar's discoveries had any importance compared with his own. However, the thought of Viar's cryptic reference to weapons returned to him. There were two remote but unpleasant possibilities there: one, that Viar might be hinting that if Krisch opposed him, he had force to back up his requests; the other, that among those weapons, just possibly, might be one whose strategic importance to Cynara would overshadow Krisch's.

It would be just as well to take care of both, and satisfy Viar at the same time, if it could be done. Krisch thought for a moment, then dictated a memo: 'Your suggestion is accepted. Send all artifacts and relevant data to this office for shipment. I will endorse your request for the establishment of a research group and will recommend your appointment as its head. In the meantime, however, I cannot authorise any further use of the Unit 1 converter for excavation purposes. Discontinue such activity, and use converter ingots pending a reply from Cynara.'

That tied it up. It was not only reasonable but accommodating; Viar could not disobey instructions without open hostility. If he did disobey, he could be dealt with; if he didn't, Krisch could end any possibility of future trouble by removing all weapons from the shipment.

There was, however, a third alternative which Krisch had not taken into account, as he discovered when he examined the crates Viar sent. They contained a considerable number and variety of artifacts, but not one of them, as far as Krisch could tell, could possibly be classed as a weapon.

It did not ring true, somehow: Viar was simply not the type to make even so definite a stand as this against a person in authority over him. He would intrigue, and he would undermine, but he would never risk his neck in open conflict. A new weapon would give him some false courage, but not, Krisch thought, that much.

A thought struck him. He said to the Pattern: 'Did you show yourself to Viar before you came to me?'

'Yes.'

'Why didn't you tell me?' Krisch gestured impatiently. 'Never mind; I know. I didn't ask you. How long did you spend and what did you discuss with him?'

'An hour and twenty minutes. I answered his questions about myself, about himself, about those who came after my makers, and about their weapons. I told him where to look for three that were in the area he was excavating.'

That was like Viar, at least, Krisch thought wryly: to get his hands on a fountainhead of power and then let go.

And Viar's sudden aggressiveness was explained. He had been shown a path to power, and the Pattern had no doubt told him a few truths about his timidity and lack of drive. Viar was, for the time being, a reformed character—and an unstable one.

The crisis was unwelcome, since it came at a time when Krisch was almost at the end of his strenuous labors; but he was realist enough to see that it had to be dealt with immediately. He considered his problem, made his preparations —which took some time, since they included transferring all big shop and laboratory equipment to the end of a half-mile tunnel dug outward from the Unit's perimeter—and then called Viar.

Viar's face was arranged in an expression of careful deference, though which cunning and self-complacency were almost obscenely visible.

Krisch cut through his greeting with, 'Viar, your instructions were to send all the artifacts to me. Where are the weapons you mentioned in your report?'

Viar's features realigned themselves to produce an effect of utter surprise. 'Why, everything's there,' he said. 'I sent it all over, just as you stipulated.'

'Viar,' said Krisch coldly, 'you unspeakable worm, guilt is written all over your face. What do you hope to gain by lying?'

Viar's white eyelashes blinked, and his weak mouth hardened slightly; but he replied in the same careful, polite tone. 'Perhaps something was left out by error, Director Krisch. Let me suggest this—send me back the items I gave you, and I'll make a careful search before I dispatch the shipment to Cynara.'

'You mean,' Krisch said, 'that I had better do as you say, or I'll get the weapons—but not in the way I expect.'

Viar's eyes gleamed. 'If you care to put it that way, Director.'

Instantly, Krisch launched himself into a torrent of abuse. He had had nine years' more experience at this form of psychological punishment than Viar, and he was a past master of the art. He called Viar a majority of filthy names in his vocabulary, with special emphasis on Viar's putative masculinity, and he delivered the whole tirade in a tone of scathing, furious contempt. He continued without slackening his pace or lowering his voice until he saw Viar redden, then turn pale; then still without a pause, he accused Viar of sabotage and treason.

Viar exploded. 'You talk about treason!' he shrieked. 'I know what you've been up to over there—I know what's been keeping you so busy! You've got that thing that escaped from my box, and you're pumping secrets out of it, to sell to the highest bidder!'

'Suppose I am?' Krisch demanded swiftly. 'What can *you* do about it?'

Viar told him. He had warned the other eight Directors that Krisch was plotting against the Project. Krisch was one against nine—he'd never get away with it—and Viar himself had a beam projector that would cut through Krisch's force screen like paper.

Krisch had all the information he needed. Now he wanted just one thing more—to get Viar out from behind the protection of his own screen. He told Viar, in extremely vulgar terms, to come and try it, and added an epithet he had been holding in reserve.

Viar's moon face went whiter than before. His eyes bulged. He opened his mouth to speak, and Krisch, grinning with triumph, cut him off.

He had been about ten minutes. He checked carefully to make sure that the Pattern was being kept occupied in the interrogation room; then he got into his battle harness and strode down the corridor toward the lift.

Halfway along the corridor was a group of cadets. One of them was on the floor, his metal body contorted and writhing. As Krisch approached, the boy began to scream at the top of his lungs. Krisch winced. He glanced at the other cadets, one of whom wore a squad leader's insignia. 'Why isn't he in surgery?' he snapped.

The squad leader said in a bewildered tone of voice, 'Surgery doesn't work, sir. The control robot there is out of commission. What shall we do, sir?'

More of the unit's services must be out than Krisch had realised; the boy evidently had some acute malfunctioning of his internal organs which should have been detected in the incipient stage by robot examiners.

'Kill him,' said Krisch, and walked on.

The voice of the squad leader followed him. 'Sir, I don't understand. Are we all going to have pain, like the lower animals?'

Krisch did not answer. He stepped into the lift at the end of the corridor and dropped swiftly to the ground level. His speedster was waiting opposite the mouth of the exit tunnel. He climbed in, worked it through the tunnel, then pointed the speedster's nose at the sky and fed it power.

Five thousand feet above the Unit's force screen and some distance away from its perimeter, he leveled off and hovered, scanning the surface below at high magnification. He waited.

There it came now: a tiny, slim, metal shape darting straight toward the Unit from the direction of Unit 1. Viar must be furious, Krisch thought. He caught the shape on the screen of his computer and snapped the controls over to 'intercept.' Instantly his craft nosed over and shot downward. He counted seconds automatically. At 'three' the other speedster was nearly in the center of his forward screen. At 'four' it entered the field of the force cannon Krisch had installed in the nose of his ship. He pressed the trigger and flung the ship into a steep ascent.

When he came out of the blackout, he saw the fragments of Viar's ship still spreading, whirling crazily under the stars. Below, an amorphous column of dust and debris was rising from the site of Unit 10. The force screen was down, and every structure above ground level had been destroyed.

Krisch leveled off and turned on the scanner that was tuned to his cavern at the end of the tunnel. It responded immediately showing him a view of the machine shop, with his nearly complete assembly standing in the middle of the room. Beyond were the transparent chambers in which the Pattern worked. Krisch saw that there were still three cadets waiting in the outer of these. It was enough. After an hour there would be no more extraneous minds to ask the Pattern questions.

Satisfied, he turned his ship toward Unit 2. It was just as well that Viar had managed to destroy Krisch's own Unit; it saved him the inconvenience of doing it himself. Neglected, the cadets had become not only distasteful but a potential danger.

He descended cautiously on Unit 2, jockeying the ship until its discharge valve was directly over the center of the force screen. Everywhere else the screen was proof against any attack likely to be mounted by a spaceship, including radioactive dust; but here, at the node, it was vulnerable to a man who knew exactly what to do. Krisch tripped the release and let the deadly stuff filter down.

He repeated the process at every remaining Unit, taking Viar's Unit 1 last. He was reasonably certain that Viar had not waited to persuade any other Director to cooperate in the attack; if he had, that Director would find nothing to attack when he got there—and no place to go when he got back.

He returned to the shambles of Unit 10, reconnoitered carefully to make sure that no other speedster was waiting within attacking range, then descended and tunneled through the debris until he struck the end of excavation. He left the speedster, opened the airtight door, one of a series that had closed when the tunnel lost air, and walked back to the cavern.

The incredibly complex structure which Krisch had built was not the final stage; it was only the final fabricator. The final product would be Krisch himself.

He experimented first with a tiny cylinder into which he had built an affinity device tuned to a target plate at the opposite end of the chamber. He lined it up so that it would pass through the field of the Pattern's machine on its way to the target, and arranged a photoelectric cell to track it and register the exact moment when it disappeared.

He released the cylinder. It streaked across the room, into the middle of the ten-foot framework of the machine—and abruptly sprouted from the target, fifty feet away. Trembling, Krisch read the meters. There was not one microsecond's difference between the time the cylinder had passed through the field and the time it had appeared on the target plate. To the limit of his equipment's ability to record, the passage had been instantaneous.

He examined the cylinder with sensitive instruments that had previously measured its dimensions, its weight and structure. The cylinder was unchanged, undistorted.

Krisch grinned at the Pattern. There was danger in that enigmatic structure of forces, he knew; but he had escaped it by a strategy that was perfect because it was so simple. There were a million questions he had wanted to ask the Pattern; they tingled within him like an internal itch; but he had not asked one. He had asked only for the technical information he needed to build the transport device—he had not even followed up any of the curious mathematical and philosophical implications of some of the steps involved.

And he knew that his certainty of safety was not self-delusion: he had checked himself daily with the hypnotically given psych tests. He was sane. His self-confidence was up a few points; that was natural. His empathy rating was down about the same amount; that had never been high—if it had, he would never have been assigned to head the Project. Those were the only changes. His orientation was perfect. There were no signs of any incipient neuroses or psychoses, including the one he had most feared: a guilt complex centered around his destruction of the cadets.

He was able to think about that without remorse, now as ever. They had only been half alive. They were better off in oblivion.

He looked at the finished device once more. It was a hollow framework of curious, out-of-plumb angles. Over it and around it crawled a metal vine bearing odd fruits: metal roses, each petal mathematically aligned; lozenges of transparent metal, each with a tiny, glowing heart. It looked like nothing so much as some alien being's notion of a work of art; but Krisch looked at it with awe and respect, remembering the labor each tiny part had cost him.

Inside, in the field created by those metal blossoms, matter gained a new dimension—permanently. It was not like the half-efficient overdrive used in spaceships—that was an artificial condition, that collapsed when the power was withdrawn. Krisch had made a visual analogy to help himself understand the difference. He imagined normal spacetime as a sphere of viscous fluid. A ship going into overdrive extended itself half out of that sphere, and tilted its molecules so that the rest offered less resistance to the liquid. But the Pattern's device extended the matter it affected like an accordion—open, half out of the stream; closed, all the way out. The matter so treated was not an uneasy visitor on the threshold of that abnormal space; it was at home there. And, once treated, it could be made to move from one space to the other at will.

It was, Krisch thought, the difference between a flying fish and an amphibian.

The test cylinder, though it now partook of the properties of both spaces, was useless for transport because it lacked control. It was set to home on the target plate where it now was. If you tried to move it away, the instant you succeeded by so much as the width of a molecule, the cylinder would return through hyperspace to its former position. The result, in gross terms, was that you simply could not budge it. It was an amusing toy, Krisch thought, and some use might later be found for it.

Target plates planted in enemy cities, for example, and radiating missiles.

But the principle military use of the device was going to involve human control. The human passenger *was* the control. You snapped into hyperspace, you selected your target in normal space, snapped through again, and you were there. In hyperspace there was a perceptible interval, long enough to choose; in normal space there was none.

Krisch checked his equipment once more. He had a semiportable field generator which projected a spherical force screen around him, and a reaction motor which could be used for short-range travel. The assembly was much too bulky and awkward to be of any use in military operations, but it was a necessary safeguard. If anything went wrong Krisch did not propose to die for want of air in interplanetary space. Also, he meant to appear somewhat dramatically in the all but impregnable fortress that housed GHQ on Cynara. A startled staff officer might conceivably turn a weapon on him before he had a chance to explain.

He considered setting a charge to destroy the Pattern's device after he had used it, and regretfully abandoned the idea. It would be good insurance against any reluctance to meet his terms, but the model itself was the only thing he had to sell. He had not drawn any plans as he worked; the plans were now in the Pattern's memory, and he had saved time by working directly from the vivid images the Pattern gave him.

Krisch turned off the power, stepped into the middle of the framework and stood with his hand on the control. There was nothing more to be done. He looked at the Pattern and thought, 'Will you be here when I return?'

'Yes.'

Good enough. The thing was not alive, not intelligent, and was therefore, obviously, incapable of boredom. Its drives took it restlessly from one questioning mind to another—when there were minds available. When there were none, it would wait. It had been built on this planet; evidently no provision had ever been made for it to leave.

It knew too much, and was intrinsically too dangerous, ever to be allowed to contact another mind. Krisch could not destroy it, but it would be here when he returned; and he could make sure that no one else would ever come to this world.

Krisch thought to himself, 'Cynara. The spaceport outside Fortress One.' He visualised it, held the thought firmly in his mind. He turned on the power.

Stunned, Krisch tried to orient himself, to figure out what was the matter. He lay weightless in a gray space, somehow above and somehow surrounded by a frightening, tangled infinity of gray spheres and white, crisscrossing lines. Everything he saw was at the same time immensely distant and so close that he could almost touch it. The array changed and shifted bewilderingly, and he tried helplessly to follow it, read some sense into its motion, until he remembered: 'Cynara. The spaceport outside Fortress One.'

There it was, below him, like some incredible four-dimensioned map, at his fingertips. He saw it clearly. He willed himself toward it, into it. But nothing happened.

Time passed, without measure. The tiny gray figures of man and machine did not move; time was suspended, for them, at the instant Krisch had entered the field. Krisch realised suddenly that he was hungry. Terrified, he looked at the dial of the airmaker at his waist. It was hard to read; the new dimension made vision queer and uncertain; but he made out at last that he had used more than three hours' supply. Time had not stopped for him.

He thought desperately, 'The Project planet. The cavern.'

Instantly, there was the cavern; the framework standing in the middle of the shop floor, and, nearby, the Pattern. An instant later the Pattern vanished.

A voice said in his mind, 'Ask me anything.'

Krisch stared at it. Was there a mocking tone in that unaccented, polite, mental voice? He said hoarsely, aloud, 'What went wrong?'

'Nothing went wrong.'

Krisch mastered himself sufficiently to say evenly, 'I was not able to enter normal space at my destination. Why not?'

'You did not wait long enough. There is a great disparity between the time rates of this plenum and the normal one; tha is why travel can be achieved at a rate which cannot be distinguished from simultaneity by your methods. In subjective terms, the trip to Cynara will take you a long time.'

'How long?' Krisch demanded. He felt helpless, fixed like a pinned specimen in the midst of this gray infinity.

'Approximately one thousand of your years.'

Krisch felt his face writhe and distort into the silent shape of a scream. Blood pounded at his temples; his eyes filmed. He said, 'How long—back to the cavern?'

'Only one year, if you were to start immediately to concentrate on the objective. If you allow yourself to drift, as you are doing now, the distance will widen rapidly.'

'But I've only got enough air for twenty hours!' Krisch shouted. 'I'll die!'

There was no response.

Krisch pulled himself back from the borderline of hysteria. He suppressed his rage and fear and uncertainty. At least—whatever the reason—the Pattern was here to answer questions. He said, 'What was your motive in lying to me?'

'I did not lie to you.'

'You told me,' Krisch said furiously, 'that there was a negligible time interval between departure and arrival. Why?'

'To me it is negligible.'

Krisch saw that it was true: it was his own fault for having phrased the question inadequately, for having refused to follow up all the implications of the science the Pattern had taught him. The Pattern, he remembered, was not alive, not intelligent—not capable of boredom.

He remembered another line of questioning that he had not followed up, and thought he saw the vague shape of a terrifying possibility.

He said, 'When you first came to me—you described yourself as a device to amuse and entertain. Was that the whole truth?'

'No.'

'What *is* the whole truth?'

The Pattern immediately began to recite the history of the race that had made it. Krisch realised petulantly that he had asked too sweeping a question, and was about to rephrase it;

but the significance of what the Pattern was saying stopped him.

They had been entirely alien, those people; their psychology was incomprehensible to men. They did not fight; they did not explore; they did not rule or exploit; they had nothing that could be identified with human curiosity—that apelike trait that had made humanity what it was. Yet they had a great science. They had acquired it for some motive that Krisch could never grasp. They had, really, only two characteristics that would be recognisable to men: they loved each other, their homes, their world; and they had a deep, joyful, ironic sense of humor.

'Men came,' said the Pattern, 'eleven million of your years ago. They wanted my makers' world and therefore they killed my makers. My makers knew anguish of flesh and spirit, but they could not fight. Aggressiveness, conflict, were inconceivable to them. But remember that they understood irony. Before the last of them died they made us as a gift to their destroyers. We were a good gift. We contain all that they knew. We were truthful. We are immortal. We are made to serve.

'It is not our makers' fault,' said the Pattern, 'if men use the knowledge we give them to destroy themselves.'

There was only a thin shred left of Krisch's hold on his sanity. He said very carefully, 'Did your makers foresee this—the situation I am in?'

'Yes.'

Is there any way for me to escape from it?

The Pattern said, 'Yes. It is the final jest of my makers. To travel in hyperspace, you must become what I am—only a pattern of forces and memory, not alive, not intelligent, not capable of boredom. I can make this alteration, if you request it. It is simple: like the growth of one crystal from another, or like the transfer of pattern in living cells.'

Krisch choked. He said, 'Will I—remember?'

'Yes. You will have your own memories in addition to those I give you. But you will not retain your human character: you will not be aggressive, or cruel, or egotistic, or curious. You will be a device for answering questions.'

Krisch's mind revolted against the thought. But he looked at the dial of his airmaker and knew what his answer would be. And in a flash of prophetic insight, he knew what would happen thereafter. He would finish his journey to Cynara. He would tell the truth, and the truth would corrupt.

Wherever there were men, throughout the universe and to the end of time, his influence would follow them. In time there would be other unwary seekers of knowledge who would take the path he had taken. By choosing this way out he would become mankind's executioner.

But when had men hesitated to risk the survival of the race for their own advantage?

The pattern, Krisch thought, was clear.

THE COUNTRY OF THE KIND

THE attendant at the car lot was daydreaming when I pulled up—a big, lazy-looking man in black satin chequered down the front. I was wearing scarlet, myself; it suited my mood. I got out, almost on his toes.

'Park or storage?' he asked automatically, turning around. Then he realised who I was, and ducked his head away.

'Neither,' I told him.

There was a hand torch on a shelf in the repair shed right behind him. I got it and came back. I knelt down to where I could reach behind the front wheel, and ignited the torch. I turned it on the axle and suspension. They glowed cherry red, then white, and fused together. Then I got up and turned the flame on both tires until the rubberoid stank and sizzled and melted down to the pavement. The attendant didn't say anything.

I left him there, looking at the mess on his nice clean concrete.

It had been a nice car, too; but I could get another any time. And I felt like walking. I went down the winding road, sleepy in the afternoon sunlight, dappled with shade and smelling of cool leaves. You couldn't see the houses; they were all sunken or hidden by shrubbery, or a little of both. That was the fad I'd heard about; it was what I'd come here to see. Not that anything the dulls did would be worth looking at.

I turned off at random and crossed a rolling lawn, went through a second hedge of hawthorn in blossom, and came out next to a big sunken games court.

The tennis net was up, and two couples were going at it just working up a little sweat—young, about half my age, all four of them. Three dark-haired, one blonde. They were evenly matched, and both couples played well together; they were enjoying themselves.

I watched for a minute. But by then the nearest two were beginning to sense I was there, anyhow. I walked down onto the court, just as the blonde was about to serve. She looked at me frozen across the net, poised on tiptoe. The others stood.

'Off,' I told them. 'Game's over.'

I watched the blonde. She was not especially pretty, as they go, but compactly and gracefully put together. She came down slowly, flat-footed without awkwardness, and tucked the racket under her arm; then the surprise was over and she was trotting off the court after the other three.

I followed their voices around the curve of the path, between towering masses of lilacs, inhaling the sweetness, until I came to what looked like a little sunning spot. There was a sundial, and a birdbath, and towels lying around on the grass. One couple, the dark-haired pair, was still in sight farther down the path, heads bobbing along. The other couple had disappeared.

I found the handle in the grass without any trouble. The mechanism responded, and an oblong section of turf rose up. It was the stair I had, not the elevator, but that was all right. I ran down the steps and into the first door I saw, and was in the top-floor lounge, an oval room lit with diffused simulated sunlight from above. The furniture was all comfortably bloated, sprawling and ugly; the carpet was deep, and there was a fresh flower scent in the air.

The blonde was over at the near end with her back to me, studying the autochef keyboard. She was half out of her playsuit. She pushed it the rest of the way down and stepped out of it, then turned and saw me.

She was surprised again; she hadn't thought I might follow her down.

I got up close before it occurred to her to move; then it was too late: She knew she couldn't get away from me; she closed her eyes and leaned back against the paneling, turning a little pale. Her lips and her golden brows went up in the middle.

I looked her over and told her a few uncomplimentary things about herself. She trembled, but didn't answer. On an impulse, I leaned over and dialed the autochef to hot cheese sauce. I cut the safety out of the circuit and put the quantity dial all the way up. I dialed *soup tureen* and then *punch bowl.*

The stuff began to come out in about a minute, steaming hot. I took the tureens and splashed them up and down the wall on either side of her. Then when the first punch bowl came out I used the empty bowls as scoops. I clotted the carpet with the stuff; I made streamers of it all along the walls, and dumped puddles into what furniture I could reach. Where it cooled it would harden, and where it hardened it would cling.

I wanted to splash it across her body, but it would've hurt, and we couldn't have that. The punch bowls of hot sauce were still coming out of the autochef, crowding each other around the vent. I punched *cancel,* and then *sauterne (swt., Calif.).*

It came out well chilled in open bottles. I took the first one and had my arm back just about to throw a nice line of the stuff right across her midriff, when a voice said behind me:

'Watch out for cold wine.'

My arm twitched and a little stream of the wine splashed across her thighs. She was ready for it; her eyes had opened at the voice, and she barely jumped.

I whirled around, fighting mad. The man was standing there where he had come out of the stair well. He was thinner in the face than most, bronzed, wide-chested, with alert blue eyes. If it hadn't been for him, I knew it would have worked—the blonde would have mistaken the chill splash for a scalding one.

I could hear the scream in my mind, and I wanted it.

I took a step toward him, and my foot slipped. I went down clumsily, wrenching one knee. I got up shaking and tight all over. I wasn't in control of myself. I screamed, 'You—you——' I turned and got one of the punch bowls and lifted it in both hands, heedless of how the hot sauce was slopping over onto my wrists, and I had it almost in the air toward him when the sickness took me—that damned buzzing in my head, louder, louder, drowning everything out.

When I came to, they were both gone. I got up off the floor weak as death, and staggered over to the nearest chair. My clothes were slimed and sticky. I wanted to die. I wanted to drop into that dark furry hole that was yawning for me an never come up; but I made myself stay awake and get out of the chair.

Going down in the elevator, I almost blacked out again. The blonde and the thin man weren't in any of the second-floor bedrooms. I made sure of that, and then I emptied the closets and bureau drawers onto the floor, dragged the whole mess into one of the bathrooms and stuffed the tub with it, then turned on the water.

I tried the third floor: maintenance and storage. It was empty. I turned the furnace on and set the thermostat up as high as it would go. I disconnected all the safety circuits and alarms. I opened the freezer doors and dialed them to defrost. I popped the stair well door open and went back up in the elevator.

On the second floor I stopped long enough to open the stairway door there—the water was halfway toward it, creeping across the floor—and then searched the top floor. No one was there. I opened book reels and threw them unwinding across the room; I would have done more, but I could hardly stand. I got up to the surface and collapsed on the lawn: that furry pit swallowed me up, dead and drowned.

While I slept, water poured down the open stair well and filled the third level. Thawing food packages floated out into the rooms. Water seeped into wall panels and machine housings; circuits and fuses blew. The air conditioning stopped, but the pile kept heating. The water rose.

Spoiled food, floating supplies, grimy water surged up the stair well. The second and first levels were bigger and would take longer to fill, but they'd fill. Rugs, furnishings, clothing, all the things in the house would be waterlogged and ruined. Probably the weight of so much water would shift the house, rupture the water pipes and other fluid intakes. It would take a repair crew more than a day just to clean up the mess. The house itself was done for, not repairable. The blonde and the thin man would never live in it again.

Serve them right.

The dulls could build another house; they built like beavers. There was only one of me in the world.

The earliest memory I have is of some woman, probably the cresh-mother, staring at me with an expression of shock and horror. Just that. I've tried to remember what happened directly before or after, but I can't. Before, there's nothing but the dark formless shaft of no-memory that runs back to birth. Afterward, the big calm.

From my fifth year, it must have been, to my fifteenth, everything I can remember floats in a pleasant dim sea. Nothing was terribly important. I was languid and soft; I drifted. Waking merged into sleep.

In my fifteenth year it was the fashion in love-play for the young people to pair off for months or longer. 'Loving steady,' we called it. I remember how the older people protested that it was unhealthy; but we were all normal juniors, and nearly as free as adults under the law.

All but me.

The first steady girl I had was named Elen. She had blonde hair, almost white, worn long; her lashes were dark and her eyes pale green. Startling eyes: they didn't look as if they were looking at you. They looked blind.

Several times she gave me strange startled glances, something between fright and anger. Once it was because I held her too tightly, and hurt her; other times, it seemed to be for nothing at all.

In our group, a pairing that broke up sooner than four weeks was a little suspect—there must be something wrong with one partner or both, or the pairing would have lasted longer.

Four weeks and a day after Elen and I made our pairing, she told me she was breaking it.

I'd thought I was ready. But I felt the room spin half around me till the wall came against my palm and stopped.

The room had been in use as a hobby chamber; there was a rack of plasticraft knives under my hand. I took one without thinking, and when I saw it I thought, *I'll frighten her.*

And I saw the startled, half-angry look in her pale eyes as I went toward her; but this was curious: she wasn't looking at the knife. She was looking at my face.

The elders found me later with the blood on me, and put me into a locked room. Then it was my turn to be frightened.

because I realised for the first time that it was possible for a human being to do what I had done.

And if I could do it to Elen, I thought, surely they could do it to me.

But they couldn't. They set me free: they had to.

And it was then I understood that I was the king of the world....

The sky was turning clear violet when I woke up, and shadow was spilling out from the hedges. I went down the hill until I saw the ghostly blue of photon tubes glowing in a big oblong, just outside the commerce area. I went that way, by habit.

Other people were lining up at the entrance to show their books and be admitted. I brushed by them, seeing the shocked faces and feeling their bodies flinch away, and went on into the robing chamber.

Straps, aqualungs, masks and flippers were all for the taking. I stripped, dropping the clothes where I stood, and put the underwater equipment on. I strode out to the poolside, monstrous, like a being from another world. I adjusted the lung and the flippers, and slipped into the water.

Underneath, it was all crystal blue, with the forms of swimmers sliding through it like pale angels. Schools of small fish scattered as I went down. My heart was beating with a painful joy.

Down, far down, I saw a girl slowly undulating through the motion of a sinuous underwater dance, writhing around and around a ribbed column of imitation coral. She had a suction-tipped fish lance in her hand, but she was not using it; she was only dancing, all by herself, down at the bottom of the water.

I swam after her. She was young and delicately made, and when she saw the deliberately clumsy motions I made in imitation of hers, her eyes glinted with amusement behind her mask. She bowed to me in mockery, and slowly glided off with simple, exaggerated movements, like a child's ballet.

I followed. Around her and around I swam, stiff-legged, first more child-like and awkward than she, then subtly parodying her motions; then improving on them until I was dancing an intricate, mocking dance around her.

I saw her eyes widen. She matched her rhythm to mine, then, and together, apart, together again we coiled the wake of our dancing. At last, exhausted, we clung together where a bridge of plastic coral arched over us. Her cool body was in the bend of my arm; behind two thicknesses of vitrin—a world away!—her eyes were friendly and kind.

There was a moment when, two strangers yet one flesh, we felt our souls speak to one another across that abyss of matter. It was a truncated embrace—we could not kiss, we could not speak—but her hands lay confidingly on my shoulders, and her eyes looked into mine.

That moment had to end. She gestured toward the surface and left me. I followed her up. I was feeling drowsy and almost at peace, after my sickness. I thought ... I don't know what I thought.

We rose together at the side of the pool. She turned to me, removing her mask: and her smile stopped, and melted away. She stared at me with a horrified disgust, wrinkling her nose.

'*Pyah!*' she said, and turned, awkward in her flippers. Watching her, I saw her fall into the arms of a white-haired man, and heard her hysterical voice tumbling over itself.

'But don't you remember?' the man's voice rumbled. 'You should know it by heart.' He turned. 'Hal, is there a copy of it in the clubhouse?'

A murmur answered him, and in a few moments a young man came out holding a slender brown pamphlet.

I knew that pamphlet. I could even have told you what page the white-haired man opened it to; what sentences the girl was reading as I watched.

I waited. I don't know why.

I heard her voice rising: 'To think that I let him *touch* me!' And the white-haired man reassured her, the words rumbling, too low to hear. I saw her back straighten. She looked across at me ... only a few yards in the scented, blue-lit air; a world away ... and folded up the pamphlet into a hard wad, threw it, and turned on her heel.

The pamphlet landed almost at my feet. I touched it with my toe, and it opened to the page I had been thinking of:

... sedation until his 15th year, when for sexual reasons it became no longer practical. While the advisors and medical staff hesitated, he killed a girl of the group by violence.

And farther down:

The solution finally adopted was three-fold.

1. *A sanction*—the only sanction possible to our humane, permissive society. Excommunication: not to speak to him, touch him willingly, or acknowledge his existence.

2. *A precaution.* Taking advantage of a mild predisposition to epilepsy, a variant of the so-called Kusko analog technique was employed, to prevent by an epileptic seizure any future act of violence.

3. *A warning.* A careful alteration of his body chemistry was affected to make his exhaled and exuded wastes emit a strongly pungent and offensive odor. In mercy, he himself was rendered unable to detect this smell.

Fortunately, the genetic and environmental accidents which combined to produce this atavism have been fully explained and can never again ...

The words stopped meaning anything, as they always did at that point. I didn't want to read any farther; it was all nonsense, anyway. I was the king of the world.

I got up and went away, out into the night, blind to the dulls who thronged the rooms I passed.

Two squares away was the commerce area. I found a clothing outlet and went in. All the free clothes in the display cases were drab: those were for worthless floaters, not for me. I went past them to the specials, and found a combination I could stand—silver and blue, with a severe black piping down the tunic. A dull would have said it was 'nice.' I punched for it. The automatic looked me over with its dull glassy eye, and croaked, 'Your contribution book, please.'

I could have had a contribution book, for the trouble of stepping out into the street and taking it away from the first passer-by; but I didn't have the patience. I picked up the one-legged table from the refreshment nook, hefted it, and swung it at the cabinet door. The metal shrieked and dented, opposite the catch. I swung once more to the same place, and the door sprang open. I pulled out clothing in handfuls till I got a set that would fit me.

I bathed and changed, and then went prowling in the big multi-outlet down the avenue. All those places are arranged pretty much alike, no matter what the local managers do to them. I went straight to the knives, and picked out three in graduated sizes, down to the size of my fingernail. Then I had to take my chances. I tried the furniture department, where I had had good luck once in a while, but this year all they were using was metal. I had to have seasoned wood.

I knew where there was a big cache of cherry wood, in good-sized blocks, in a forgotten warehouse up north at a place called Kootenay. I could have carried some around with me—enough for years—but what for, when the world belonged to me?

It didn't take me long. Down in the workshop section, of all places, I found some antiques—tables and benches, all with wooden tops. While the dulls collected down at the other end of the room, pretending not to notice, I sawed off a good oblong chunk of the smallest bench, and made a base for it out of another.

As long as I was there, it was a good place to work, and I could eat and sleep upstairs, so I stayed.

I knew what I wanted to do. It was going to be a man, sitting, with his legs crossed and his forearms resting down along his calves. His head was going to be tilted back, and his eyes closed, as if he were turning his face up to the sun.

In three days it was finished. The trunk and limbs had a shape that was not man and not wood, but something in between: something that hadn't existed before I made it.

Beauty. That was the old word.

I had carved one of the figure's hands hanging loosely, and the other one curled shut. There had to be time to stop and say it was finished. I took the smallest knife, the one I had been using to scrape the wood smooth, and cut away the handle and ground down what was left of the shaft to a thin spike. Then I drilled a hole into the wood of the figurine's hand, in the hollow between thumb and curled finger. I fitted the knife blade in there; in the small hand it was the sword.

I cemented it in place. Then I took the sharp blade and stabbed my thumb, and smeared the blade.

I hunted most of that day, and finally found the right place —a niche in an outcropping of striated brown rock, in a little triangular half-wild patch that had been left where two roads forked. Nothing was permanent, of course, in a community like this one that might change its houses every five years or so, to follow the fashion; but this spot had been left to itself for a long time. It was the best I could do.

I had the paper ready: it was one of a batch I had printed up a year ago. The paper was treated, and I knew it would stay legible a long time. I hid a little photo capsule in the back of the niche, and ran the control wire to a staple in the base of the figurine. I put the figurine down on top of the paper, and anchored it lightly to the rock with two spots of all-cement. I had done it so often that it came naturally; I knew just how much cement would hold the figurine steady against a casual hand, but yield to one that really wanted to pull it down.

Then I stepped back to look: and the power and the pity of it made my breath come short, and tears start to my eyes.

Reflected light gleamed fitfully on the dark-stained blade that hung from his hand. He was sitting alone in that niche that closed him in like a coffin. His eyes were shut, and his head tilted back, as if he were turning his face up to the sun.

But only rock was over his head. There was no sun for him.

Hunched on the cool bare ground under a pepper tree, I was looking down across the road at the shadowed niche where my figurine sat.

I was all finished here. There was nothing more to keep me, and yet I couldn't leave.

People walked past now and then—not often. The community seemed half deserted, as if most of the people had flocked off to a surf party somewhere, or a contribution meeting, or to watch a new house being dug to replace the one I had wrecked.... There was a little wind blowing toward me, cool and lonesome in the leaves.

Up the other side of the hollow there was a terrace, and on that terrace, half an hour ago, I had seen a brief flash of color—a boy's head, with a red cap on it, moving past and out of sight.

That was why I had to stay. I was thinking how that boy might come down from his terrace and into my road, and passing the little wild triangle of land, see my figurine. I was thinking he might not pass by indifferently, but stop: and go closer to look: and pick up the wooden man: and read what was written on the paper underneath.

I believed that sometime it had to happen. I wanted it so hard that I ached.

My carvings were all over the world, wherever I had wandered. There was one in Congo City, carved of ebony, dusty-black; one on Cyprus, of bone; one in New Bombay, of shell; one in Chang-teh, of jade.

They were like signs printed in red and green, in a color-blind world. Only the one I was looked for would ever pick one of them up, and read the message I knew by heart.

TO YOU WHO CAN SEE, the first sentence said, I OFFER YOU A WORLD....

There was a flash of color up on the terrace. I stiffened. A minute later, here it came again, from a different direction: it was the boy, clambering down the slope, brilliant against the green, with his red sharp-billed cap like a woodpecker's head.

I held my breath.

He came toward me through the fluttering leaves, ticked off by pencils of sunlight as he passed. He was a brown boy, I could see at this distance, with a serious thin face. His ears stuck out, flickering pink with the sun behind them, and his elbow and knee pads made him look knobby.

He reached the fork in the road, and chose the path on my side. I huddled into myself as he came nearer. *Let him see it, let him not see me*, I thought fiercely.

My fingers closed around a stone.

He was nearer, walking jerkily with his hand in his pockets, watching his feet mostly.

When he was almost opposite me, I threw the stone.

It rustled through the leaves below the niche in the rock. The boy's head turned. He stopped, staring. I think he saw the figurine then. I'm sure he saw it.

He took one step.

'Risha!' came floating down from the terrace.

And he looked up. 'Here,' he piped.

I saw the woman's head, tiny at the top of the terrace. She called something I didn't hear; I was standing up, tight with anger.

Then the wind shifted. It blew from me to the boy. He whirled around, his eyes big, and clapped a hand to his nose.

'Oh, what a stench!' he said.

He turned to shout, 'Coming!' and then he was gone, hurrying back up the road, into the unstable blur of green.

My one chance ruined. He would have seen the image, I knew if it hadn't been for that damned woman and the wind shifting.... They were all against me, people, wind and all.

And the figurine still sat, blind eyes turned up to the rocky sky.

There was something inside me that told me to take my disappointment and go away from there, and not come back.

I knew I would be sorry. I did it anyway: took the image out of the niche, and the paper with it, and climbed the slope. At the top I heard his clear voice laughing.

There was a thing that might have been an ornamental mound, or the camouflaged top of a buried house. I went around it, tripping over my own feet, and came upon the boy kneeling on the turf. He was playing with a brown and white puppy.

He looked up with the laughter going out of his face. There was no wind, and he could smell me. I knew it was bad. No wind, and the puppy to distract him—everything about it was wrong. But I went to him blindly anyhow, and fell on one knee, and shoved the figurine at his face.

'Look——' I said.

He went over backwards in his hurry: he couldn't even have seen the image, except as a brown blur coming at him. He scrambled up, with the puppy whining and yapping around his heels, and ran for the mound.

I was up after him, clawing up moist earth and grass as I rose. In the other hand I still had the image clutched, and the paper with it.

A door popped open and swallowed him and popped shut again in my face. With the flat of my hand I beat the vines around it until I hit the doorplate by accident and the door opened. I dived in, shouting, 'Wait,' and was in a spiral passage, lit pearl-gray, winding downward. Down I went headlong, and came out at the wrong door—an underground conservatory, humid and hot under the yellow lights, with dripping rank leaves in long rows. I went down the aisle raging, overturning the tanks, until I came to a vestibule and an elevator.

Down I went again to the third level and a labyrinth of guest rooms, all echoing, all empty. At last I found a ramp leading upward, past the conservatory, and at the end of it voices.

The door was clear vitrin, and I paused on the near side of it looking and listening. There was the boy, and a woman old enough to be his mother, just—sister or cousin, more likely—and an elderly woman in a hard chair holding the puppy. The room was comfortable and tasteless, like other rooms.

I saw the shock grow on their faces as I burst in: it was always the same, they knew I would like to kill them, but they never expected that I would come uninvited into a house. It was not done.

There was that boy, so close I could touch him, but the shock of all of them was quivering in the air, smothering, like a blanket that would deaden my voice. I felt I had to shout.

'Everything they tell you is lies!' I said. 'See here—here, this is the truth!' I had the figurine in front of his eyes, but he didn't see.

'Risha, go below,' said the young woman quietly. He turned to obey, quick as a ferret, I got in front of him again. 'Stay,' I said, breathing hard. 'Look——'

'Remember, Risha, don't speak,' said the woman.

I couldn't stand any more. Where the boy went I don't

134

know; I ceased to see him. With the image in one hand and the paper with it, I leaped at the woman. I was almost quick enough; I almost reached her; but the buzzing took me in the middle of a step, louder, louder, like the end of the world.

It was the second time that week. When I came to, I was sick and too faint to move for a long time.

The house was silent. They had gone, of course ... the house had been defiled, having me in it. They wouldn't live here again, but would build elsewhere.

My eyes blurred. After a while I stood up and looked around the room. The walls were hung with a gray close-woven cloth that looked as if it would tear, and I thought of ripping it down in strips, breaking furniture, stuffing carpets and bedding into the oubliette.... But I didn't have the heart for it. I was too tired. Thirty years.... They had given me all the kingdoms of the world, and the glory thereof, thirty years ago. It was more than one man alone could bear, for thirty years.

At last I stooped and picked up the figurine, and the paper that was supposed to go under it—crumpled now, with the forlorn look of a message that someone has thrown away unread.

I sighed bitterly.

I smoothed it out and read the last part.

YOU CAN SHARE THE WORLD WITH ME. THEY CAN'T STOP YOU. STRIKE NOW—PICK UP A SHARP THING AND STAB, OR A HEAVY THING AND CRUSH. THAT'S ALL. THAT WILL MAKE YOU FREE. ANYONE CAN DO IT.

Anyone. Someone. Anyone.

TICKET TO ANYWHERE

I

RICHARD FALK was a sane man. Up until three months ago he had been, so far as he could discover, the only sane man left in a world of lunatics.

Now he was a dead man.

He lay in a metal coffin twenty yards long by three wide, airless, soundless. Behind the faceplate of his helmet, under the rime of frozen air, his lips were bright blue, his cheeks, nose, forehead a lighter color, almost violet. The flesh was stiff as frozen leather. He did not move, breathe, or think: he was dead.

Beside him, strapped to the bulging torso of his suit, was a metal box labeled: SCATO HEART PROBE. SEE INSTRUCTIONS INSIDE.

All around him, strapped tight to the walls by broad loops of webbing, were boxes, canisters, canvas bags, kegs. Cargo. His coffin was a freighter, going to Mars.

In his frozen brain the memories were neatly stacked, just as he had left them. Not coupled now, each cell isolated, the entropy of his mind fallen to zero. But uppermost among them, waiting for the thaw that might never come, were the memories of his last few hours of life.

Once the ship was launched and free, he had had to wait until its dancing molecules had stilled, their heat all radiated away into space. Then to wait again, heater turned off, listening to the silence while his own life's heat drained away: fingers and toes numb first, ears and nose following, then lips, cheeks, and all his flesh; shivering in an agony of cold, watching his breath fill the helmet with cloud, the cold drops beading on the colder faceplate.

Tricky, that, and a thing that demanded courage. Act too soon, and the last drop into stillness would be too slow—the freezing liquids in his body would crystallize, gashing his cells with a million tiny stabs. Wait too long, and the cold would stead his ability to act at all.

He had waited until the false warmth of the dying had crept over him, the subtle destroyer, cumbering his limbs not with harshness but with too much peace. Twisting then in the dead center where he floated, he had drawn himself into the lane between two looped bundles of cargo, forcing them aside, until he reached the naked hull. There, spread-eagled against the chill metal, embracing it as one who crucifies himself gladly, he had died.

The ship, stillest of sepulchers, hung fixed in the center of the starry globe. So it might have remained for time without end, changeless, knowing no time; for there was no time here, no 'events'—the ship and all its contents—except its robot control, inactive now but warmed by a minute trickle of electrons—now being very nearly at zero Absolute.

But a relay clicked, communicating its tremor through support frame and girder and hull. Time had begun again. The radar assembly in the prow began to emit timed clusters of radiation; presently other relays snapped over, and then the engine awoke, whispered to itself an instant, and was silent. For an instant the ship had become once more a thing in motion, a pebble flung between the stars. Another such instant came, then another; then, at long last, the hull shuddered to the whip and carom of atmospheric molecules. Lightly it dipped into Martian air, out again, in again, making a great circuit of the globe. A final relay clicked, and Falk's coffin hurled itself groundward, free of the skeletal ship whose rockets now flamed again, driving it back into the timeless deep.

A parachute opened as the cargo hull hurtled downward: a preposterous parasol that would not have held the weight a minute against Earth's gravity, in Earth's air; but here it slowed that plummeting fall until the box met Martian sand at not quite killing speed.

In the shell, Falk's corpse slowly thawed.

His heart was beating. That was Falk's first conscious realisation, and he listened to the tiny sound thankfully. His chest was rising and falling in a deep, slow rhythm; he heard the hiss and whisper of breath in his nostrils and felt the veins twitch at his temples.

Then came a prickling, half pain, in his arms and legs; then he saw a ruddy haze of light on his closed lids.

Falk opened his eyes.

He saw a pale glow that turned itself into a face. It went away briefly, and came back. Falk could see it a little better now. Young—about thirty—pale-skinned, with a blue beard shadow. Black straight hair, a little untidy. Black-rimmed spectacles. Ironic lines on either side of the thin mouth.

'All right now?' said the face.

Falk murmured, and the face bent closer. He tried again. 'Think so.'

The young man nodded. He picked up something from the bed and began taking it apart, fitting the components into the cushioned troughs of a metal box. It was the heart probe, Falk saw: the bulky control box and the short, capillary-thin needle.

'Where did you get this?' the young man asked. 'And what the devil were you doing aboard that freighter?'

'Stole the probe,' said Falk. 'And the suit, and the rest of the stuff. Dumped enough cargo to match my weight. Wanted to get to Mars. Only way.'

The young man let his hands fall into his lap. 'You *stole* it,' he repeated incredulously. 'Then you never had the analogue treatment?'

Falk smiled. 'Had it, all right. Dozen times. Never took.' He felt very tired. 'Let me rest a minute, will you?'

'Of course. Sorry.'

The young man went away, and Falk closed his eyes, returning to the slow surge of memory that moved in his mind. He went through those last hours, painful as they were, and then again. There was trauma there; mustn't let it get buried to cause him trouble later. Accept it, know the fear, live with it.

After a while the young man came back, carrying broth that steamed in a cup, and Falk drank it gratefully. Then he fell unknowing into sleep.

When he awoke he was stronger. He tried to sit up, and found to his mild surprise that he could. The other, who had been sitting in an armchair across the room, put down his pipe and came over to thrust pillows behind Falk's back. Then he sat down again. The room was cluttered and had a stale odor. Floor, walls and ceiling were enameled metal. There were books and rolls of tape, records, in shelves; more piled on the floor. A dirty shirt was hanging from the doorknob.

'Want to talk now?' the young man asked. 'My name's Wolfert.'

'Glad to know you. Mine's Falk.... You want to know about the analogue business first, I suppose.'

'And why you're here.'

'It's the same thing,' Falk told him. 'I'm immune to analogue treatment. I didn't know it for sure till I was ten, but I think I was born that way. From seven on, I remember the other kids talking about their Guardians, and me pretending I had one too. You know how kids are—anything to run with the mob.

'But for a long time, years, I wasn't certain whether everyone else was pretending like me, or whether I really was the only one without an invisible Guardian to talk to. I was pretty sure the kids were lying when they said they could see theirs, but whether they were there at all or not was another question. I didn't know; actually it didn't bother me much.

'When I was ten, I stole something. It was a book I wanted that my father wouldn't let me have. The clerk was looking the other way—I put it under my jacket. Funny, I was halfway through it before it struck me that I'd just proved I had no Guardian. By that time, you see, I'd decided that I'd just never seen mine because I'd never done anything bad. I was proud of that, a little prissy about it if you want the truth—only I wanted this book....

'I had sense enough, thank God, to burn that book after I'd finished it. If I hadn't, I don't suppose I would have lived to grow up.'

Wolfert grunted. 'Should think not,' he said. His eyes were fixed on Falk, interested, alert, wary. 'One man without any control could turn the whole applecart over. But I thought immunity was theoretically impossible?'

'I've thought about that a good deal. According to classic psychology, it is. I'm not unusually resistant to hypnotic drugs; I go under all right. But the censor mechanism just doesn't respond. I've had the fanciful notion that I may be a mutation, developed in response to the analogue treatment as an anti-survival factor. But I don't know. As far as I've ever been able to find out, there are no more like me.'

'Umm,' said Wolfert, puffing at his pipe. 'Should think your next move would be to get married, have children, see if they were immune too.'

Falk stared at him soberly. 'Wolfert—no offense, but can you imagine yourself settling down happily in a community of maniacs?'

The other's face flushed slowly. He took his pipe out of his mouth, looked down at it. Finally he said, 'All right, I know what you mean.'

'Maybe you don't,' said Falk, thinking, *I've offended him. Couldn't help it.* 'You've been out here ten years, haven't you?'

Wolfert nodded.

'Things are getting worse,' Falk told him. 'I've taken the trouble to look up some statistics. They weren't hard to find; the damned fools are proud of them. The number of persons in mental institutions has gone steadily down since 1980, when the world-wide analogue program got under way. Extension of analogue program, steadily up. The two curves cancel out perfectly.

'There are fewer and fewer people that have to be put away in madhouses—not because of any improvement in therapy, but because the analogue techniques are getting better and better. The guy who would have been hopelessly insane fifty years ago now has a little man inside his head, steering him around, making him act normal. On the outside he *is* normal; inside, he's a raving madman. Worse still, the guy who would have been just a little bit cracked fifty years ago—and gotten treatment for it—is now just as mad as the first guy. It doesn't matter any more. We could all be maniacs, and the world would go on just as before.'

Wolfert grimaced wryly. 'Well? It's a peaceful world, any-how.'

'Sure,' said Falk. 'No war or possibility of war, no murders, no theft, no crime at all. That's because every one of them has a policeman inside his skull. But action begets reaction, Wolfert, in psychiatry as well as in physics. A prison is a place to get out of, if it takes you a lifetime. Push one plunger down, another will rise. Just a few years more, I think—ten or twenty, say—and you'll see that madhouse curve rise again. Because there's no escape from the repression of the Guardians except a further retreat into insanity. And eventually a point is reached where no amount of treatment can help. What are they going to do then?'

Wolfert tamped his pipe out slowly and stood up, sucking absently at the stem. 'You say *they*,' he said, 'meaning the psychiatrists who really govern Earth, I suppose. You've evidently figured out what you're going to do.'

Falk smiled. 'Yes. With your help—I'm going to the stars.'

The other stood frozen a moment. 'So you know about that,' he said. 'Well—— Come into the next room. I'll show it to you.'

Falk had known about the Doorway, but not that it looked like this. It was a cubicle of something that looked like slick brown glass. Ten feet high, six wide and deep. Inside, at waist level on the far wall, a lever—curiously shaped, like the head of an old-fashioned walking stick, the slightly curved bar of the L parallel to the wall. Nothing more than that. The floor of Wolfert's hut had been assembled around it. It was the reason for the hut's existence, for Wolfert's dearly bought presence on Mars.

'So that's it,' said Falk. He took a step toward it.

'Stay where you are,' Wolfert said sharply. 'The area in front of the entrance is booby-trapped.'

Falk stopped and looked at Wolfert, then at the metal cabinets bolted to the floor on either side of the Doorway. Now that he looked at them closely, he could see the lenses of black-light beams and, above them, metal cones that he supposed were discharge points.

Wolfert confirmed it. 'If anything ever comes out, the

current is supposed to get him. If it doesn't, I'm here.' He put his hand on the rapid-fire automatic at his belt.

Falk sat down slowly on a bench next to the wall. 'Why?' he asked. 'Why are they so afraid of whatever might come out of the Doorway?'

The other leaned awkwardly against the wall and began re-filling his pipe. 'You don't know the whole story, then,' he said. 'Tell me what you do know, and I'll fill in the gaps.'

Falk said slowly, 'I was able to find out that the Doorway existed—that the first Mars expedition, in '76 had found it here. Apparently it was known to be an interstellar trans-portation system, but as far as I could learn nobody had ever actually tried it out. I knew that a caretaker had been left here—your predecessor, I take it—after the idea of colonising Mars was abandoned. But I didn't know any of the reasons.'

Wolfert grinned briefly and straightened away from the wall. As he talked, he paced back and forth across the room, glancing at Falk only occasionally. 'It's a transportation sys-tem, all right. Put an object in that cubicle, press the lever down—the object vanishes. So does most of the crowbar or whatever you use to work the lever. *FffT*—gone.

'We don't know how old it is and have no way of telling. The material it's made of is harder than diamond. About half of it is underground. That was the way it was found—sitting perfectly level on the surface of the desert. I believe it must have some sort of self-leveling mechanism built into it so that it's always available no matter what happens to the surface.

'Other ruins have been found on Mars, but they're all stone and quite primitive; nothing like this. The first expedition tried to get into its innards and find out what made it go, of course, but they couldn't. You can *see* in, but there's nothing to see.' He gave his quick, bitter smile. 'It's frustrating. Makes a physicist feel like a backward student in a kindergarten.

'We know that it's part of an interstellar network. One man did try it out—a member of the first expedition, one of the group that found the Doorway in the first place. He saw the cubicle and the lever—stepped in and pressed it to find out what would happen. *He* found out, all right, but I don't sup-pose the rest of us will ever know. The second expedition brought along a batch of powerful all-wave senders and sent them through. They picked up the first signal five years later, from the general direction of Regulus. Two more after seven years, then four during the thirteenth year, all from different directions. The other eight have yet to be heard from.'

He stopped pacing and looked at Falk. 'Now do you understand? The thing has no selectivity—it's completely random. We could walk through here and step out onto the planet of another star, all right—but it would take us a million years to find the way back by trial and error.' He knocked his pipe out against the heel of his hand, letting the dottle fall on the floor. 'There it sits, the doorway to the stars. And we can't use it.'

Falk leaned back against the wall, trying to absorb the idea. 'Maybe there are only a dozen or so stars in the network,' he suggested.

Wolfert's thin mouth drew down at the corners. 'Don't be a fool,' he said. 'Would the race that could build *that*'—he gestured toward the cubicle—'stop at a dozen stars, or a thousand? The devil! They owned the galaxy!' Nervously he began to fill his pipe again. 'Sixty billion stars,' he said. 'And according to current theory, all the mainliners have planets.'

He pointed to the cubicle again. 'Three hundred sixty cubic feet, about,' he said. 'Enough for one man and supplies for a month, or fifteen people and supplies for a week. That's the limit of the size of the colony we could send out. With no assurance,' he added bitterly, 'that they'd land anywhere they could live for a minute.'

'Frustrating,' Falk agreed. 'But I still don't see why you're here—with a gun. I can understand that if a member of the race that built that thing came through—and I must say it seems unlikely—that would be an important event. But why kill him when he steps out?'

'Dammit,' said Wolfert violently, 'it isn't my policy, Falk. I only work here.'

'I understand that,' Falk said. 'But do you have any idea what's behind the policy?'

'Fear,' said Wolfert promptly. 'They've got too much at stake.' He leaned against the wall again, gesturing with his pipestem. 'Do you realise,' he said, 'that we could have interstellar colonisation *without* this gadget, on our own? Certainly. Not now, but fifty, a hundred years from now—if we worked at it. Give us a fuel source efficient enough so that we can accelerate continuously for as long as eight months, and we could reach the stars well within a man's lifetime. But do you know why we won't?

'They're afraid. They're even afraid to plant colonies here on Mars, or on Jupiter's moons, simply because transportation takes too long. Imagine a colony cut off from Earth by a five- or ten-year trip. Say something goes wrong—a man like yourself, naturally immune to analogue treatment. Or a man who somehow evades the treatment, then manages to take it over, change it. Say he cuts out the one directive, "You must do nothing against the policy or interests of Earth." Then you've got two communities again, not one. And then——?'

Falk nodded soberly. 'War. I see now. They don't dare take even the smallest chance of that.'

'It isn't a question of daring, they *can't*. That's one of the directives in their own conditioning, Falk.'

'So we'll never get to the stars.'

'Unless,' said Wolfert, 'somebody walks out of that Doorway who understands how it works. The voltage is high, but not high enough to kill—we hope. He's supposed to be stunned. If the current doesn't stop him, and he tries to get back into the Doorway, I'm supposed to shoot to cripple. But at all events, he's supposed to be stopped. He isn't to be allowed to go back and warn others to stay away from this station. Because if we had that knowledge—how to alter the system so that it would be selective——'

'Then we'd have colonies, all right,' finished Falk. 'Every one just around the corner from Earth. All just alike. The loonies shall inherit the Universe.... I hope nobody ever comes through.'

'I don't think you're likely to be disappointed,' said Wolfert.

II

He prowled the rest of the cabin with Wolfert, resting at intervals until his strength returned. There wasn't much to see: the Doorway room, with a spyhole Falk had not noticed between it and the bedroom; the room that housed radio, radar, and the computer that controlled the grazing orbits of the supply rockets; the power plant, and the compressor that kept the cabin's air at breathable pressure; kitchen, bathroom, and two storage chambers.

The radio room had a window, and Falk stood there a long time, looking out over the alien desert, violet now as the sun dropped toward the horizon. Stars glittered with unfamiliar brilliance in the near-black sky, and Falk found his gaze drawn to them even against the tug of that unearthly landscape.

In his mind he sketched hairlines of fire across the sky—a cat's cradle of stars. The thought that tomorrow he would be standing on a planet of one of those suns was like an icy douche; the mind recoiled from it as from the thought of personal death. But at the same time it lured him. He felt like a boy standing on the edge of an unsounded pool whose black water might hold treasure or death: he was afraid to dive, and yet he knew that he must.

How could a man feel otherwise, he wondered, knowing that the way was open, that he had only to step forward?

Wolfert said abruptly, 'You haven't asked me whether I reported to Earth when I found you in that freighter shell.'

Falk looked at him. 'You did, of course,' he said. 'It doesn't matter. I'll be gone long before they can do anything about me. You'll tell them that I overpowered you and escaped through the Doorway—they won't be able to prove otherwise —unless you're conditioned against lying?'

'No,' said Wolfert, 'I'm not. That part's all right, with one mendation: I'll say I revived you, then shot and buried you. But what made you so sure that I'd be—sympathetic?'

'You're here,' said Falk simply. 'You're a volunteer. They haven't got to the stage of conditioning people to do jobs they don't want to do, though I suppose they will eventually. And then I'd heard you speak, I knew you were intelligent. So— you're a hermit. You don't like the madhouse they're making out of Earth, any more than I do.'

'I don't know,' said Wolfert slowly. 'Perhaps you're assuming too much similarity.' He looked down at his ever-present

pipe, tamping the tobacco with a horny thumb: 'I don't feel as
you do about the analogue system, or the present government.
I'm—adjusted, there. In my personal universe, it works. I can
see that it will lead to disaster eventually, but that doesn't
bother me much. I'll be dead.'

He looked at Falk earnestly. 'But I want the stars,' he said.
'That's an emotional thing with me.... There are no slugs in
these cartridges.' He indicated the gun at his hip. 'Or in any of
the ammunition I've got. They didn't condition me against
that.'

Falk stared at him. 'Look,' he said abruptly, 'you've got a
directive against stepping through that Doorway, is that
right?'

The other nodded.

'Well, but is there any reason why I couldn't knock you over
the head and drag you through?'

Wolfert smiled wryly, shaking his head slowly. 'No good,'
he said. 'Somebody's got to stay, this end.'

'Why?'

'Because there's a chance that you'll find the secret out
there, somewhere. That's what you're hoping, too, isn't it?
You're not just looking for a place to hide—you could do that
in a thousand places on Earth. You're after knowledge, and in
spite of what I've told you, you're hoping you'll be able to
bring it back and make the Earth over.'

'It sounds a little quixotic,' said Falk, 'but you're right.'

Wolfert shrugged, letting his gaze drift away again. 'Well
then ... there's got to be somebody here. Somebody with no
slugs in his gun. If I went with you, they'd take good care to
send a different sort of man next time.'

He met Falk's eyes briefly. 'Don't waste time feeling sorry
for me,' he said. 'You may not believe it, but I'm quite happy
here. When I'm ... alone, that is.'

Falk had been wondering why the government had not sent
a married couple instead of a single man, who might go mad
from sheer loneliness. Now it struck him that he had been
stupid. Wolfert had a wife, undoubtedly; the best kind—one
who suited him perfectly, who would never be fickle, or want
to return to Earth; one who cost nothing to feed, consumed no

146

air, and had not added an ounce of weight when Wolfert had been shipped out here. And on Mars it did not ordinarily matter that no one else could see her.

He felt an inward twinge of revulsion and instantly knew that Wolfert had seen and understood it. The man's cheeks flushed, and he turned away to stare through the window, his lips thin and hard.

After a moment Falk said, 'Wolfert, I like you better than any man I've ever met. I hope you'll believe that.'

Wolfert hauled out a pipe cleaner, a complicated thing of many hinged stems, the free ends stamped into shovel shapes, tamper, shapes, probes. He said, 'I'm afraid I dislike you, Falk, but it's nothing personal. I simply hate your guts a little, because you've got something I wasn't lucky enough to be born with. You're the master of your own mind.'

He turned and put out his hand, grinning. 'Aside from that trifling matter, I entirely approve of you. If that's good enough——?'

Falk gripped his hand. 'I hope you're here when I get back,' he said.

'I'll be here,' said Wolfert, scraping his pipe, 'for another thirty-odd years, barring accidents. If you're not back by then, I don't suppose you'll be coming back at all.'

At Wolfert's suggestion, Falk put on one of the other's light Mars suits instead of the spacesuit he had worn in the freighter. The latter, designed for heavy-duty service in the orbital space station that circled Earth, was, as Wolfert pointed out, too clumsy for use on a planet's surface. The lighter suit furnished adequate protection in thin atmosphere and was equipped with gadgetry that the other lacked: a head lamp, climbing gear, built-in compasses, and traps for the occupant's ingestion and excretion. It carried air tanks, but also had a compression outfit—which, given an atmosphere at least as oxygen-rich as that of Mars, would keep the wearer alive for as long as the batteries held out.

'You'll have to find a place where you can live off the land, so to speak, anyhow,' said Wolfert. 'If all the planets you hit should happen to be dead, so will you be, very shortly. But this suit will give you longer to look, at least, and the stuff in the knapsack will last you as long as you have air. I'd give you this gun, but it wouldn't do you any good—all the ammunition's dud, as I told you.'

He disconnected the booby trap and stood aside as Falk moved to the entrance. Falk took one last look around at the bare metal room and at Wolfert's spare figure and gloomy face. He stepped into the brown-glass cubicle and put his gloved hand on the lever.

'See you later,' he said.

Wolfert nodded soberly, almost indifferently. 'So long, Falk,' he said, and put his pipe back in his mouth.

Falk turned on his helmet lamp, put his free hand near the control box at his belt—and pressed the lever down.

Wolfert vanished. An instant later Falk was aware that the lever was no longer beneath his hand. He turned, dazedly, and saw that it was back in its original position, above his hand.

Then he remembered the curious blank that had taken Wolfert's place and he turned again to the entrance. He saw—nothing. A gray-white blankness, featureless, uncommunicative. Was this some kind of intermediary state—and if so, how long did it last? Falk felt a brief surge of panic as he realised they had only assumed the journey was instantaneous, and another as he recalled the eight transmitters that had never been heard from. . . .

Then common sense took over, and he stepped forward to the entrance.

The gray-white shaded gradually, as his gaze traveled downward, into gray-blue and violet, and then a chaos of dim colors of which his eye made nothing. He gripped the edge of the Doorway and bent forward, looking downward and still downward. Then he saw the cliff, and all the rest of the scene fell into perspective.

He stood at the top of a sheer mountain—an impossible, ridiculous height. Down it went and again down, until whatever was at the bottom melted into a meaningless tapestry of grayed color. He looked to right and left and saw nothing else. No sound came through the diaphragm of his helmet. He had only the tactile and muscular responses of his own body, and he hard reality of the Doorway itself, to assure him that he was real and live.

The planet was dead; he felt irrationally sure of that. It *felt* dead; there was not even a whisper of wind: only the featureless blanket of gray cloud, the cliff, the meaningless colors below.

He looked at the kit slung to his belt: the pressure gauge, bottled litmus papers, matches. But there was no point in testing this atmosphere: even if it were breathable, there was nearly no way of getting out of the Doorway. The cliff began not more than an inch from the entrance.

Falk went back to the lever, pressed it down again.

This time he watched it as it reached the end of its stroke. There was no hint of a transition: the lever was there, under his hand, and then it was back in the starting position—as if it had passed unfelt through the flesh of his hand.

He turned.

Deep blue night, blazing with stars. Underneath, a flat blue-green waste that ran straight away into the far distance.

Falk stepped out onto the icy plain and looked around him, then upward. The sky was so like the one he had known as a boy in Michigan that it struck him almost as a conviction that his terminus was on Earth—in the Antarctic, perhaps, near the pole, where no explorer had ever happened across it. Then, as he looked automatically for the Dipper, Orion's Belt, he knew that he was wrong.

He saw none of the familiar patterns. These were alien stars, in an alien sky. He reviewed what he could remember of the configurations of Earth's southern hemisphere, but none of them fitted either.

Directly above him was a group of eight stars, two of them very brilliant—four arranged in a straight line, the rest spread out in an almost perfect semicircle. Falk knew that if he had ever seen that constellation before he would not have forgotten

Now he looked down toward the horizon, blacker than the sky. How could he know that light, warmth, safety, knowledge were not hiding just beyond the curve of the planet?

He turned back to the cubicle. He was here on sufferance, a

man in a Mars suit, with weeks—or, with great luck, months or years—to live. He had to find what he sought within a pitifully small radius from the Doorway, or not at all.

Down went the lever again. Now it was still night—but when Falk went to the Doorway, he saw an avenue of great buildings under the stars.

Now the pressure gauge came out—low, but the compressor could handle it. The litmus papers—negative. The match burned—weakly, and only for an instant, but it burned.

Falk started the compressor and shut off the flow of air from the tanks slung at his back. Then he turned on his helmet light and marched off down the avenue.

The buildings were variations on a theme: pyramid, cone and wedge shape, they sloped away as they rose, so that for all their enormous bulk they did not hide the sky. Falk looked up when he had taken a few steps, subconsciously expecting to see the half-circle constellation. But it was not there, and he realised with a shock that, for all he knew, he might be halfway across the galaxy from the spot where he had stood five minutes ago.

He drew a picture of the galaxy in his mind, an oval clot of mist against blackness. Near one focus of the ellipse he put a dot of brightness that stood for Sol. Then he made another dot and drew a shining line between them. Then another dot, and another line; then another. They made a sprawling letter N across the misty oval.

It was incomprehensible. A race that could span the galaxy but could not choose one destination from another?

The only other alternative was: there was some function of the Doorways that men had failed to grasp, some method of selection had evaded them, as a savage might be bewildered in a modern tubeway system. But Falk's mind rejected that. The mechanism was simple and clear. A cubicle and a lever. Function is expressed by shape; and the shape of the Doorway said 'Go'; it did not say 'Where?'

He looked again at the buildings. The upper quarter of them, he saw now, was badly eroded: layers inches deep had been eaten away. He glanced at the fine orange sand that paved the avenue and saw that it filled doorways almost to the top. Evidently this city had lain all but buried for many years, and in some recent time the shifting sands had uncovered it again.

The space between the sand and the tops of the doorways was narrow, but he thought he could squeeze through. He picked out one, centering it in the brilliant disk of his head lamp—and stood there, in the middle of the avenue, reluctant to move.

He glanced back at the cubicle, as if for reassurance. It was still there, comfortably clear and sharp-lined, timeless. Now he realised what was troubling him. This city was dead—dead as the planet of the cliff or the planet of ice. The buildings were stone; they had crumbled under the weather. Their makers were dust.

He had agreed with Wolfert when the other had suggested that he was on a quest for knowledge; that he hoped the Doorway would eventually take him back to Sol, armed with knowledge, ready to remake the world. But it wasn't true. That had been his conscious idea, but it was a dream, a self-delusion—an excuse.

He had no love for Earth, or any conviction that humanity must be rescued from its own weakness. If that force had driven him, there would have been no logic in leaving Earth. He could have stayed, worked himself into the governing elite, organised a revolution from within. His chance of success would have been small, but there would have been some chance.

Yes, he might have done it—and for what? To remove the one control that kept humanity from destroying itself?

That coin had the same face on both sides. Uncontrolled, mankind was not fit to colonise. Controlled, it dared not take the risk. Human civilisation was not ready, was a dead end, an aborted experiment. Mankind was a dirty beast, ravaging its planet, befouling itself—capable of any imaginable perversion, degradation, horror.

But there had been another civilisation once—one that had been worthy of the stars. Falk did not believe it was dead. Stone crumbled; metal rusted; and the races that used them vanished and were not mourned. The Doorways still lived, still functioned, defying time.

That race was not here; it had left no trace of itself except the Doorway. Without another glance at the buildings around him, Falk turned and went back to the brown glass cubicle.

When he was three yards away from it, he saw the footprints.

There were five of them, lightly impressed into the sand near the Doorway's entrance. Search as he might, Falk could not find any more. Two, apparently, pointed away from the cubicle; the other three were the returning trail, for one overlapped one of the previous set.

They were smaller than Falk's booted prints, oval, slightly flattened along the sides. Falk stared at them as if the mere act of looking would make them give up more information; but they told him nothing.

They were not human; but what did that prove?

They had been made long since the time when the Doorways had been built; Falk did not know what winds swept this world, but it could only have been a few years, at most, since the sands had dropped to their present level. But even that train of logic led nowhere.

They could be the trace of a Doorway builder. Or they could have been made by a wanderer like himself, another barbarian venturing in the paths of his betters.

The bitterest thing of all was that, having found the trail, he could not follow it. For it led through the Doorway—to any one of sixty billion suns.

Falk stepped into the cubicle and pressed the lever down once more.

III

White light that sealed his eyes with pain, and a vicious torrent of heat. Gasping, Falk groped frantically for the lever.

The afterimage faded slowly. He saw night again, and the stars. The last one, he thought, must have been the planet of a nova. How many of those was he likely to run into?

He stepped to the doorway. A wasteland: not a stick, not a stone.

He went back to the lever. Light again, of bearable intensity, and a riot of color outside.

Falk stepped cautiously to the entrance. Slowly his mind adapted to the unfamiliar shapes and colors. He saw a bright landscape under a tropic sun—gray-violet mountains in the distance, half veiled by mist; nearer, tall stalks that bore heavy leaves and fronds of startling blue-green; and directly ahead of him, a broad plaza that might have been cut from one monstrous boulder of jade. On either side were low, box-shaped structures of dark vitreous material: blue, brown, green and red. And in the middle of the plaza stood a group of slender shapes that were unquestionably alive, sentient.

Falk's heart was pounding. He stepped behind the shelter of the entrance hall and peered out. Curiously it was not the cluster of live things that drew him, but the buildings on either side.

They were made of the same enduring, clean-edged substance as the Doorway. He had come, by blind chance, at last to the right place.

Now he stared at the creatures grouped in the middle of the plaza. For some reason they were disappointing. They were slender S-shapes, graceful enough in repose: lizard shapes, upright on two legs; pink of belly and umber of back. But in spite of the bandoliers slung from their narrow shoulders, in spite of their quick patterned gestures as they spoke together, Falk could not convince himself that he had found the people he sought.

They were too manlike. One turned away while two others spoke; came back leaning at a passionate angle, thrust himself between the two, gesturing wildly. Shouted down, he again left and stalked a half circle around the group. He moved as a chicken moves, awkwardly, thrusting his long neck forward at each step.

Of the five others, two argued, two merely stood with drooping, attentive heads and watched; and the last stood a little apart, gazing around him disdainfully.

They were funny, as monkeys are funny—because they resemble men. We laughed at our mirrored selves. Even the faces of man laugh at each other when they should weep.

153

They're tourists, Falk thought. *One wants to go to the Lido,* *another insists they see the Grand Canal first; the third is* *furious with both of them for wasting time, the next two are* *too timid to interfere, and the last one doesn't care.*

He couldn't imagine what their reaction to him would be. Nothing welcome, at any rate; they might want to take him home as a souvenir. He wanted to get into those buildings, but he'd have to wait until they were out of sight.

While he waited, he got out the atmosphere-testing kit. The pressure gauge showed the merest trifle less than Earth normal; the litmus papers did not react; the match burned cheerfully, just as it would have on Earth. Falk turned off the oxygen, cracked the helmet valve cautiously, and sniffed.

After the stale air of the suit, the breath he inhaled was so good that it brought tears to his eyes. It was fresh, faintly warm, and sweet with flower fragrance. Falk opened the helmet seam, tipped the helmet back, and let the breeze wash over his face and hair.

He peered out, and saw to his dismay that the party was trooping directly toward him. Falk ducked his head back inside, glanced instinctively at the lever, then looked out again.

They were running now; they had seen him. They ran very clumsily, heads darting strenuously forward and back. The one in the lead was opening and shutting his triangular mouth, and Falk heard faint yawps. He leaped out of the cubicle, cut sharply to the right, and ran.

The nearest building with a visible opening, unfortunately, was some distance down the line, between Falk and the lizards. He glanced back when he was halfway there. The lizards were considerably strung out now, but the leader was only a few yards away.

They were faster than they looked. Falk put his head down and tried to make his heavy boots move to a quicker rhythm. Almost to the door, he looked back again. The lizard was one jump away, its grimy, ball-tipped fingers outspread.

Falk turned in desperation and, as the lizard came up, swung a knotted fist to the point of its snout. He heard a steam-whistle screech, saw it collapse, and then he was diving through the open door ahead.

The door closed gently behind him—a sheet of glassy substance, the same blue as the walls, gliding down to seal the opening.

Falk stared at it. Through its transparency he could see the dark shapes of the lizards crowding around, leaning to pry at the bottom of the door, gesticulating at each other. It was plain, at any rate, that the door was not going to open for them.

Whether it would open for him, when he wanted it to, was another matter.

He looked around him. The building was a single huge room, so long and deep that he could barely see the far walls. Scattered over the floor, patternless, were boxes, or chests, racks, shelves, little ambiguous mounds. Nearly all the objects Falk could see were fashioned of the same glass-like material.

There was no dust in the room; but now that Falk thought of it, he realised that there had been none in any of the Doorways, either. How that was done he could not conjecture. He moved to the nearest object, a file, or rack formed apparently to take many things of diverse shapes and sizes. It was a quarter empty now, and the remaining contents had a jumbled look.

He picked up an orange glass spindle, full of embedded threads, or flaws that looped in a curious pattern from one end to the other. He put it down, took a hollow sphere of opal. It was made in halves and seemed to be empty, but Falk could find no way to take it apart. He replaced it and took a brown object shaped like a double crescent, with a clear fracture plane running diagonally through it. . . .

Half an hour later he realised that he was not going to find any picture books or engineering manuals or any one thing that would unlock the mystery of the Doorway people for him. If there were any knowledge to be gained here, it would have to come from the building as a whole.

The lizards distracted him. He could see them through the walls of the building, pressing their snouts against the glass, staring with little round eyes, gesturing at him. But he learned things from them.

155

The group broke up finally, leaving only one to guard the exit; the others dispersed. Falk saw one go into the building directly across the plaza. The door closed behind him. A little later another one approached and pounded on the door; but it did not open until the first lizard came close to it inside. Some automatic mechanism, beyond Falk's fathoming, evidently responded to the presence or absence of any living thing inside each building. When the last person left, the door stayed open; when another person entered, it shut and would not open for the next unless the first person allowed it.

That added one item to the description of the Doorway people that Falk was building in his mind. They were not property-conscious—not afraid that thieves would enter in their absence, for the doors stood open when they were gone—but they respected each other's love of privacy.

Falk had previously thought of this building as a vast factory or laboratory or dormitory—a place designed to serve a large number of people, anyhow. Now he revised his opinion. Each building, he thought, was the private domain of one person—or, if they had family groups, only two or three. But how could one person use all this space, all these possessions?

He made the comparison that by now was becoming automatic. He asked himself what a cliff dweller would make of a millionaire's triplex apartment in New York.

It helped, but not enough. The objects around him were all specialised tools; they would not function for him and so told him nothing about the Doorway builders. There was nothing that he could compare to a bed, to a table, to a shower bath. He could not see the people who had lived here.

With an effort, he forced himself to stop thinking in terms of men. The facts were important, not his prejudices. And then what had been a barrier became a road. There were no beds, tables, showers? Then the Doorway people did not sleep; they did not eat; they did not bathe.

Probably, thought Falk, they did not die.

They were fit to live among the stars....

The riddle of the deserted chamber mocked him. How, having built this city, would they leave it? How would they

156

spread the network of the Doorways across the face of the galaxy, and then leave it unused?

The first question answered itself. Looking at the littered chamber, Falk thought of his comparison of the cliff dweller and the millionaire and humbly acknowledged his presumption. Not a millionaire's triplex, he told himself ... a tent.

Once there had been something of particular interest on this world. No telling what it had been, for that had been some millions of years ago when Mars was a living world. But the Doorway people, a few of them, had come here to observe it. When they were finished, they had gone away, leaving their tents behind, as a man might abandon a crude shelter of sticks and leaves.

And the other things they had left behind them? The cubes, cones, rods, odd shapes, each one beyond price to a man? *Empty cans*, thought Falk; *toothpaste tubes, wrapping paper*.

They had abandoned this city and the million things in it because they were of no value.

The sun was redder, nearer the horizon. Falk looked at the chronometer strapped to the wrist of his suit and found to his surprise that it was more than five hours since he had left Volfert on Mars.

He had not eaten. He took food out of his pack and looked at the labels on the cans. But he was not hungry; he did not even feel tired.

He watched the lizards outside. They were scurrying around in the plaza now, bringing armloads of junk from the building, packing them into big red boxes. As Falk watched, a curious construction floated into view down at the end of the plaza. It was a kind of airboat, an open shell with two lizards riding it, supported by two winglike extensions with streamlined, down-pointing shapes at their ends.

It drifted slowly until it hovered over the pile of boxes the lizards had gathered. Then a hatch opened in its belly, and a hook emerged at the end of three cords. The lizards on the plaza began slinging loops of cord from their boxes to the hook.

Falk watched them idly. The hook began to rise, dragging

157

the boxes after it, and at the last moment one of the lizards
tossed another loop over it.

The new box was heavy; the hook stopped when it took up
the slack, and the airboat dipped slightly. Then it rose again,
and the hook rose too, until the whole load was ten feet off the
ground.

Abruptly one of the three cords snapped; Falk saw it whip
through the air, saw the load lurch ponderously to one side
and the airboat dip. Simultaneously the pilot sent the boat
down to take up the strain on the remaining cords.

The lizards were scattering. The load struck heavily; and a
moment later so did the airboat. It bounced, skidded wildly
and came to rest as the pilot shut off the power.

The lizards crowded around again, and the two in the airboat climbed down for an interminable conference. Eventually
they got aboard again, and the boat rose a few feet while the
lizards beneath disengaged the hook. Then there was another
conference. Falk could see that the doors of the boat's hatch
were closed and had a crumpled look. Evidently they were
jammed and could not be opened again.

Finally the boat came down once more, and with much
argument and gesticulation the boxes were unpacked and some
of their contents reloaded into two boxes, these being hoisted
with much effort into the airboat's cockpit. The rest was left
strewn around the plaza.

The airboat lifted and went away, and most of the lizards
followed it. One straggler came over for a last look at Falk; he
peered and gestured through the wall for a while, then gave it
up and followed the rest. The plaza was deserted.

Some time passed, and then Falk saw a pillar of white flame
that lifted, with a glint of silver at its tip, somewhere beyond
the city, and grew until it arched upward to the zenith,
dwindled, and vanished.

So they had spaceships, the lizards. They did not dare use
the Doorways, either. Not fit, not fit . . . too much like men.

Falk went out into the plaza and stood, letting the fresher-
ing breeze ruffle his hair. The sun was dropping behind the
mountains, and the whole sky had turned ruddy, like a great
crimson cape streaming out of the west. Falk watched, re-

luctant to leave, until the colors faded through violet to gray, and the first stars came out.

It was a good world. A man could stay here, probably, and live his life out in comfort and ease. No doubt there were exotic fruits to be had from those trees; certainly there was water; the climate was good; and Falk thought sardonically that there could be no dangerous wild beasts, or those twittering tourists would never have come here.

If all a man wanted was a hiding place, there could be no better world than this. For a moment Falk was strongly tempted. He thought of the cold dead world he had seen and wondered if he would ever find a place as fair as this again. Also, he knew now that if the Doorway builders still lived, they must long ago have drawn in their outposts. Perhaps they lived now on only one planet, out of all the billions. Falk would die before he found it.

He looked at the rubble the lizards had left in the middle of the plaza. One box was still filled, but burst open; that was the one that had caused all the trouble. Around it was a child's litter of baubles—pretty glass toys, red, green, blue, yellow, white.

A lizard, abandoned here by his fellows, would no doubt be happy enough in the end.

With a sigh, Falk turned back to the building. The door opened before him, and he collected his belongings, fastened down his helmet, strapped on his knapsack again.

The sky was dark now, and Falk paused to look up at the familiar sweep of the Milky Way. Then he switched on his helmet light and turned toward the waiting Doorway.

The light fell across the burst box the lizards had left, and Falk saw a hard edge of something thrusting out. It was not the glassy adamant of the Doorway builders; it looked like stone.

Falk stooped and tore the box aside.

He saw a slab of rock, roughly smoothed to the shape of a wedge. On its upper face, characters were incised. They were in English.

With blood pounding in his ears, Falk knelt by the stone and read what was written there.

THE DOORWAYS STOP THE AGING PROCESS. I WAS 32 WHEN I LEFT MARS, AM HARDLY OLDER NOW THOUGH I HAVE BEEN TRAVELING FROM STAR TO STAR FOR A TIME I BELIEVE CANNOT BE LESS THAN 20 YEARS. BUT YOU MUST KEEP ON. *I* STOPPED HERE 2 YRS. FOUND MYSELF AGING—HAVE OBSERVED THAT MILKY WAY LOOKS NEARLY THE SAME FROM ALL PLANETS SO FAR VISITED. THIS CANNOT BE COINCIDENCE. BELIEVE THAT DOORWAY TRAVEL IS RANDOM ONLY WITHIN CONCENTRIC BELTS OF STARS & THAT SOONER OR LATER YOU HIT DOORWAY WHICH GIVES ENTRY TO NEXT INNERMOST BELT. IF I AM RIGHT, FINAL DESTINATION IS CENTER OF GALAXY. I HOPE TO SEE YOU THERE.

JAMES E. TANNER
NATIVE OF EARTH

Falk stood up, blinded by the glory of the vision that grew in his mind. He thought he understood now why the Doorways were not selective and why their makers no longer used them.

Once—a billion years ago, perhaps—they must have been uncontested owners of the galaxy. But many of their worlds were small planets like Mars—too small to keep their atmospheres and their water forever. Millions of years ago, they must have begun to fall back from these. And meanwhile, Falk thought, on the greater worlds just now cooling, the lesser breeds had arisen: the crawling, brawling things. The lizards. The men. Things not worthy of the stars.

But even a man could learn if he lived long enough, journeyed far enough. James Tanner had signed himself not 'TERRAN SPACE CORPS' or 'U.S.A.' but 'NATIVE OF EARTH.'

So the way was made long, and the way was made hard; and the lesser breeds stayed on their planets. But for a man, or a lizard, who would give up all that he called 'life' for knowledge, the way was open.

Falk turned off the beam of his lamp and looked up at the diamond mist of the galaxy. Where would he be a thousand years from today? Standing on that mote of light, or that, or that . . . ?

Not dust, at any rate. Not dust, unmourned, unworthy. He

would be a voyager with a destination, and perhaps half his journey would be done.

Wolfert would wait in vain for his return, but it would not matter; Wolfert was happy—if you called that happiness. And on Earth, the mountains would rise and fall long after the question of human survival had been forgotten.

Falk, by that time, perhaps, would be home.

BEACHCOMBER

MAXWELL and the girl with the astonishing bust had started their weekend on Thursday in Venice. Friday they went to Paris, Saturday to Nice, and on Sunday they were bored. The girl, whose name was Alice, pouted at him across the breakfast table. 'Vernon, let's go someplace else,' she said.

'Sure,' said Maxwell, not too graciously. 'Don't you want your bug eggs?'

'Urgh,' said Alice, pushing them away. 'If I ever did, I don't now. Why do you have to be so unpleasant in the morning?'

The eggs were insect eggs, all right, but they were on the menu as *oeufs Procyon Thibault*, and three of the half-inch brown spheres cost about one thousand times their value in calories. Maxwell was well paid as a script writer for the North American Unit Ministry of Information—he bossed a gang of six gagmen on the Cosmic Cocktail show—but he was beginning to hate to think about what these five days were costing him.

Maxwell was a small man, sturdily built and not bad-looking, except that he was a little pop-eyed. When he raised his eyebrows, which he did whenever he spoke, his brown forehead creased into accordionlike wrinkles. Some girls found this attractive; those who didn't were usually impressed by his hand-finished duroplast tunics and forty-credit cummerbunds. He had an unhappy suspicion that Alice, whose most prominent feature has already been mentioned, was one of the latter group.

'Where do you want to go?' asked Maxwell. Their coffee came out of the conveyor, steaming and fragrant, and he sipped his moodily. 'Want to run over to Algiers? Or up to Stockholm?'

'No,' said Alice. She leaned forward across the table and
162

put up one long white hand to keep her honey-colored hair out of her eyes. 'You don't know what I mean. I mean, let's go to some other planet.'

Maxwell choked slightly and spilled coffee on the table top. 'Europe is all right,' Alice was saying with disdain, 'but it's all getting to be just like Chicago. Let's go some place different for once.'

'And be back by tomorrow noon?' Maxwell demanded. 'It's ten hours even to Proxima; we'd have just time to turn around and get back on the liner.'

Alice dropped her long lashes, contriving to look inviting and sullen at the same time. Not bad at that, Maxwell thought, for ten o'clock in the morning. 'You couldn't get Monday off, I suppose,' she said.

Maxwell's crew worked two weeks ahead, anyhow; it would only mean digging in harder when he got back. What the hell, why not play sick until Tuesday or Wednesday?

Alice's lashes rose again, slowly enough for one swift, sure look at Maxwell's face. Then her eye corners crinkled, and she gave him her A-Number-One smile. '*That's* why I love you so, Vernie,' she said with satisfaction.

They took the liner to Gamma Tauri IV, the clearing point for the system, then transferred to the interplanet shuttle for Three. Three was an almost undeveloped planet; there were perhaps a hundred cities near the equator, and some mines and plantations in the temperate zones—the rest was nothing but scenery. Maxwell had heard about it from people at the Ministry; he'd been warned to go within a year or so if he went at all—after that it would be as full of tourists as Proxima II.

The scenery was worth the trip. Sitting comfortably on their rented airscooters, stripped to shorts and shirts, with the polarised sunscreens moderating the blazing heat of Gamma Tauri, Maxwell and the girl could look in any horizontal direction and see a thousand square miles of exuberant blue-green foliage.

Two hundred feet below, the tops of gigantic tree ferns waved spasmodically in the breeze. They were following a chain of low mountains that bisected this continent; the treetops sloped away abruptly on either side, showing an occasional glimpse of reddish-brown undergrowth, and merged into a sea of blue-green that became bluer and mistier toward the horizon. A flying thing moved lazily across the clear, cumulus-dotted sky, perhaps half a mile away. Maxwell trained his binoculars on it: it was an absurd lozenge with six pairs of wings—an insect, perhaps; he couldn't tell. He heard a raucous cry down below, not far away, and glanced down hoping to see one of the carnivores; but the rippling sea of foliage was unbroken.

He watched Alice breathing deeply. Maxwell grinned. Her face was shiny with perspiration and pleasure. 'Where to now?' he asked.

The girl peered to the right, where a glint of silver shone at the horizon. 'Is that the sea over there?' she asked. 'If it is, let's go look for a nice beach and have our lunch.'

There were no nice beaches; they were all covered with inch-thick pebbles instead of sand; but Alice kept wanting to try the next place. After each abortive approach, they went up to two thousand feet to survey the shore line. Alice pointed and said, 'There's a nice-looking one. Oh! There's somebody on it.'

Maxwell looked, and saw a tiny figure moving along the shore. 'Might be somebody I know,' he said, and focused his binoculars. He saw a broad, naked back, dark against the silvery sea. The man was stooping, looking at something on the beach.

The figure straightened, and Maxwell saw a blazing crest of blond hair, then the strongly modeled nose and chin, as the man turned. 'Oh-oh,' he said, lowering the binoculars.

Alice was staring intently through her binoculars. 'Isn't he handsome,' she breathed. 'Do you know him?'

'Yes,' said Maxwell. 'That's the Beachcomber. I interviewed him a couple of times. We'd better leave him be.'

Alice kept staring. 'Honestly,' she said. 'I never saw such a—— Look, Vernie, he's waving at us.'

Maxwell looked again. The Beachcomber's face was turned up directly toward them. As Maxwell watched, the man's lips moved unmistakably in the syllables of his name.

Maxwell shortened the range, and saw that the Beach-comber was indeed waving. He also saw something he had missed before: the man was stark naked.

'He's recognised me,' he said, with mingled emotions. 'Now we'll have to go down.'

Alice took her eyes away from the binoculars for the first time since they had sighted the man. 'That's silly,' she said. 'How could he—— Vernon, you don't mean he can see us clearly from that far away?'

Maxwell waved back at the tiny figure and mouthed silently, 'Coming right down. Put some pants on, dammit.' He said to Alice, 'That's not all he can do. Weren't you listening when I said he's the Beachcomber?'

They started down on a long slant as the little figure below moved toward the jungle's edge. 'The who?' said Alice, look-ing through the binoculars again.

'Watch where you're going,' said Maxwell, more sharply than he had intended.

'I'm sorry. Who is he, dear?'

'The Beachcomber. The Man From the Future. Haven't you seen a newscast for the last five years?'

'I only tune in for the sports and fashions,' Alice said abstractedly. Then her mouth formed an O. 'My goodness! Is *he* the one who——'

'The same,' said Maxwell. 'The one who gave us the inertialess drive, the anti-friction field, the math to solve the three-body problem, and about a thousand other things. The guy from three million years in the future. And the loneliest man in all creation, probably. This is the planet he showed up on, five years ago, now that I come to think of it. I guess he spends most of his time here.'

'But why?' asked Alice. She looked toward the tiny beach, which was now vacant. Her expression, Maxwell thought, said that there were better uses to which he could put himself.

Maxwell snorted. 'Did you ever read——' He corrected himself; Alice obviously never read. 'Did you ever see one of the old films about the South Seas? Ever hear of civilised men going native" or becoming beachcombers?'

Alice said, 'Yes,' a trifle uncertainly.

'All right, imagine a man stranded in a universe full of savages—pleasant, harmless savages, maybe, but people who are three million years away from his culture. What's he going to do?'

'Go native,' said Alice, 'or comb beaches.'

'That's right,' Maxwell told her. 'His only two alternatives. And either one is about as bad as the other, from his point of view. Conform to native customs, settle down, marry, lose everything that makes him a civilised man—or just simply go to hell by himself.'

'That's what he's doing?'

'Right.'

'Well, but what is he combing those beaches *for*?'

Maxwell frowned. 'Don't be a cretin. These particular beaches have nothing to do with it; he just happens to be on one at the moment. He's a beachcomber because he lives like a bum—doesn't do any work, doesn't see people, just loafs and waits to be old enough to die.'

'That's awful,' said Alice. 'It's—such a waste.'

'In more ways than one,' Maxwell added drily. 'But what do you want? There's only one place he could be happy—three million years from now—and he can't go back. He says there isn't any place to go back to. I don't know what he means; he can't explain it any better than that, apparently.'

The Beachcomber was standing motionless by the edge of the forest as their scooters floated down to rest on the pebbly beach. He was wearing a pair of stained, weathered duroplast shorts, but nothing else; no hat to protect his great domed head, no sandals on his feet, no equipment, not even a knife at his belt. Yet Maxwell knew that there were flesh-eaters in the jungle that would gobble a man, outside the force field of his scooter, in about half a second. Knowing the Beachcomber, none of this surprised him. Whether it occurred to Alice to be surprised at any of it, he couldn't tell. She was eating the Beachcomber with her eyes as he walked toward them.

Maxwell, swearing silently to himself, turned off his scooter's field and stepped down. Alice did the same. *I only hope she can keep from trying to rape him*, Maxwell thought

166

Aloud, he said, 'How's it, Dai?'

'All right,' said the Beachcomber. Up close, he ceased to be merely impressive and became a little frightening. He stood over seven feet tall, and there was an incredible strength in every line of him. His clear skin looked resilient but *hard*; Maxwell privately doubted that you could cut it with a knife. But it was the eyes that were really impressive: they had the same disquieting, alien quality as an eagle's. Dai never pulled his rank on anybody; he 'went native' perfectly when he had to, for social purposes; but he couldn't help making a normal human adult feel like a backward child.

'Dai, I'd like you to meet Alice Zwerling.' The Beachcomber acknowledged the introduction with effortless courtesy; Alice nearly beat herself to death with her eyelashes.

She managed to stumble very plausibly as they walked down to the water's edge, and put a hand on the giant's arm for support. He righted her casually with the flat of his hand on her back—at the same time giving a slight push that put her a step or two in advance—and went on talking to Maxwell.

They sat down by the water's edge, and Dai pumped Maxwell for the latest news on Earth. He seemed genuinely interested; Maxwell didn't know whether it was an act or not, but he talked willingly and well. The Beachcomber threw an occasional question Alice's way, just enough to keep her in the conversation. Maxwell saw her gathering her forces, and grinned to himself.

There was a pause in Maxwell's monologue, and Alice cleared her throat. Both men looked at her politely. Alice said, 'Dai, are there really man-eating animals in this jungle? Vernon says so, but we haven't seen one all the time we've been here. And——' Her gaze ran down the Beachcomber's smooth, naked torso, and she blushed very prettily. 'I mean——' she added, and stopped again.

The Beachcomber said, 'Sure, there are lots of them. They don't bother me, though.'

She said earnestly, 'You mean—you walk around, like that, in the jungle, and nothing can hurt you?'

'That's it.'

Alice drove the point home. 'Could you protect another person who was with you, too?'

'I guess I could.'

Alice smiled radiantly. 'Why, that's too good to be true! I was just telling Vernon, before we saw you down here, that I wished I could go into the jungle without the scooter, to see all the wild animals and things. Will you take me in for a little walk, Dai? Vernon can mind the scooters—you wouldn't mind, would you, Vernie?'

Maxwell started to reply, but the Beachcomber forestalled him. 'I assure you, Miss Zwerling,' he said slowly, 'that it would be a waste of your time and mine.'

Alice blushed again, this time not so prettily. 'Just what do you mean?' she demanded.

Dai looked at her gravely. 'I'm not quite such a wild man as I seem,' he said. 'I always wear trousers in mixed company.' He repeated, with emphasis, '*Always.*'

Alice's lips grew hard and thin, and the skin whitened around them. Her eyes glittered. She started to say something to the Beachcomber, but the words stuck in her throat. She turned to Maxwell. 'I think we'd better go.'

'We just got here,' Maxwell said mildly. 'Stick around.'

She stood up. 'Are you coming?'

'Nope,' said Maxwell.

Without another word she turned, walked stiffly to her scooter, got in and soared away. They watched the tiny shining speck dwindle and disappear over the horizon.

Maxwell grinned, a little sickly, and looked at the Beachcomber. 'She had that coming,' he said. 'Not that she's out anything—she's got her return ticket.' He put a hand behind him to hoist himself to his feet. 'I'll be going now, Dai. Nice to have——'

'No, stay a while, Vern,' said the giant. 'I don't often see people.' He looked moodily off across the water. 'I didn't spoil anything special for you, I hope?'

'Nothing special,' Maxwell said. 'Only my current light o' love.' The giant turned and stared at him, half frowning.

'What the hell!' said Maxwell disgustedly. 'There are plenty of other pebbles on the beach.'

'Don't say that!' The Beachcomber's face contorted in a blaze of fury. He made a chopping motion with his forearm. Violent as it was, the motion came nowhere near Maxwell. Something else, something that felt like the pure essence of wrath, struck him and bowled him over, knocking the breath from him.

He sat up, a yard away from the giant, eyes popping foolishly. 'Whuhh——' he said.

There was pain and contrition in the Beachcomber's eyes. 'I'm sorry,' he said. He helped Maxwell to sit up. 'I don't often forget myself that way. Will you forgive me?'

Maxwell's chest was still numb; it was hard to breathe. 'Don't know,' he said with difficulty. 'What did you do it for?'

Sunlight gleamed dazzlingly on the Beachcomber's bare head. His eyes were in deep shadow, and shadows sketched the bold outline of his nose, marked the firm, bitter lines of his mouth. He said, 'I've offended you.' He paused. 'I'll explain, Vernon, but there's one condition—don't tell anybody else, ever.'

He put his big hand on Maxwell's wrist and Maxwell felt the power that flowed from him. 'All right?'

'All right,' said Maxwell. A curious complex of emotions boiled inside him—anger and petulance, curiosity, and something else, deeper down: a vague, objectless fear. 'Go ahead.'

The Beachcomber talked. After a few minutes he seemed almost to forget Maxwell; he stared out across the silver sea, and Maxwell, half hypnotised by the deep, resonant voice, watched his hawklike profile in silence.

Dimly, he saw the universe the Beachcomber spoke of: a universe of men set free. Over that inconceivable gap of time that stretched between Maxwell's time and theirs, they had purged themselves of all their frailties. Maxwell saw them striding among the stars, as much at home in the pitiless void as on the verdant planets they loved. He saw them tall and faultless and strong, handsome men and beautiful women, all with the power that glowed in the Beachcomber, but without a hint of his sadness. If they were angels, he was Lucifer.

He tried to imagine what the daily life of those people must be like, and couldn't; it was three million years beyond his comprehension. But when he looked at the Beachcomber's face, he knew that the last men were human beings like himself, capable of love, hate, joy and despair.

'We had mating customs that would seem peculiar to you,' said the Beachcomber after a while. 'Like elephants—because we were so long-lived, you know. We—married—late, and it was for life. My marriage was about to take place when we found the enemy.'

'The enemy?' said Maxwell. 'But—didn't you say you were the only dominant life form in the whole universe?'

'That's right.' The Beachcomber outlined an egg-shaped figure with a motion of his cupped hands, caressingly. 'The universe; all of it. Everything that existed in this space. It was all ours. But the enemy didn't come from this universe.'

'Another dimension?' Maxwell asked.

The Beachcomber looked puzzled. 'Another——' he said, and stopped. 'I thought I could say it better than that in English, but I can't. Dimension isn't right—call it another time-line; that's a little closer.'

'Another universe like ours, co-existent with this one, anyhow,' said Maxwell.

'No—not the same as ours, at all. Different laws, different——' He stopped again.

'Well, can you describe the enemy?'

'Ugly,' said the Beachcomber promptly. 'We'd been searching other—dimensions, if you want to use that word—for thousands of years, and this was the first intelligent race we found. We hated them on sight.' He paused. 'If I drew you a picture, it would look like a little spiny cylinder. But a picture wouldn't convey it. I can't explain.' His mouth contracted with distaste.

'Go on,' said Maxwell. 'What happened? They invaded you?'

'No. We tried to destroy them. We broke up the crystal spiderwebs they built between their worlds; we smashed their suns. But more than a quarter of them survived our first attack, and then we knew we were beaten. They were as powerful as we were, more so in some ways——'

'Wait, I don't get it,' said Maxwell unbelievingly. 'You—attacked them—without provocation? Wiped out three-quarters of them, simply because——'

'There was no possible peace between us and them,' said the Beachcomber. 'And it was only a matter of time before they discovered us; it was simply a chance that we made the contact first.'

What would an unspoiled South Sea Islander have made of the first atomic war? Maxwell wondered. Morals of one society didn't apply to another, he knew. Still—was it possible that the Beachcomber's people, Maxwell's own descendants, still had a taint of the old Adam? And was it accident that they were the only dominant life form in the entire universe, or had they eliminated all other contenders?

Not for him to judge, he decided; but he didn't like it. He said, 'Then what? They counterattacked?'

'Yes. We had time to prepare, and we knew what they were going to do. The trouble was, there simply was no defense against it.' He noticed Maxwell's wry smile. 'Not like the planet busters; there is a defense against those, you just haven't found it yet. But there actually was no defense whatever against their weapon. They were going to destroy our universe, down to the last quantum—wipe it right out of the series, make a blank where it had been.'

'And?' said Maxwell. He was beginning to understand why the Beachcomber had never told this story to anyone else; why the public at large must never know it. There was a feeling of doom in it that would color everything men did. It was possible, he supposed, to live with the knowledge that the end of it all was death, but fatalism was the mark of a dying culture.

'And there was just one thing we could do,' said the Beachcomber. 'Not a defense, but a trick. At the instant before their weapon was due to take effect, we planned to bring our universe back three million years along its own time-line. It would vanish, just as if it had been destroyed. Then, if it worked, we'd be able to return, but on a different time-line—because, obviously, on our own line nothing like this doubling back had already happened. Changing the past changes the future; you know the theory.'

'Yeah. So—you were too late, is that it? You got away, but all the rest were destroyed.'

'The timing was perfect,' said the Beachcomber. 'All the calculations were perfect. There's a natural limit to the distance in time any mass can travel, and we managed to meet it exactly. Three million years. I wish we hadn't. If we hadn't, I could go back again——' He stopped, and his jaw hardened.

'There isn't much more to tell,' he said. 'I happened to be chosen to execute the plan. It was a great honor, but not an easy one to accept. Remember, I was about to be married. If anything went wrong it meant that we'd be separated forever.... We couldn't even die together. But I accepted. I had one day with her—one day; and then I set up the fields and waited for the attack. Just one microsecond before it would have reached us, I released the energy that was channeled through me—and the next instant, I was falling into the ocean out there.'

He turned a tormented face to Maxwell. 'It was the worst possible luck!' he said. 'You can see for yourself, there was less chance of my landing anywhere near a planet than of— finding one given pebble on all the beaches of this planet.'

Maxwell felt as if he had missed the point of a joke. 'I still don't understand,' he said. 'You say *you* landed—but what about the universe? Where did it——'

The Beachcomber made an impatient gesture. 'You don't think we could bring it back into a space it already occupied, do you? It was in stasis, all but a fraction out of this time-line. Just a miniature left, so that it could be controlled. A model of the universe, so big.' He spread his thumb and forefinger an inch apart. 'Just a pebble.'

Maxwell's jaw dropped open. He stared at the giant. 'You don't mean—you——'

'Oh, yes,' said the Beachcomber. 'I landed about twenty miles out from shore—five years ago.' He stared out across the sea, while his fingers groped nervously among the pebbles at his feet.

'And when I hit the water,' he said, 'I dropped it.'

CLIFFORD D. SIMAK
Way Station

As keeper of the way station, Enoch Wallace was the only human privileged to communicate with the rest of the galaxy. He looked like any other man on Earth, except that he was 124 years old and showed no signs of aging. And his house seemed like any other, though mysteriously impregnable. All was quiet around Enoch's isolated farm – until someone raided the family graveyard and discovered an unknown horror.

Time is the Simplest Thing

For thirty hours he had roamed the alien planet. All around was a howling wilderness of sand. Suddenly Blaine realized he had entered some sort of dwelling place. The floor was hard and smooth, and of a bright blue colour. And then he saw the life – the thing that sprawled limply on the floor. Fully twelve feet high, it was pink, an exciting pink. And it was aware of him.

He sensed the flutter of a thought half-formed, and had to fight down the elation that surged inside him, for it was seldom that one contacted a telepathic creature.

Hang on, he told himself, hang on!

And the creature spoke.

Hi, pal, it said. *I trade with you my mind.*

ANDREW J. OFFUTT
Messenger of Zhuvastou

A novel of Heroic Fantasy

In hot pursuit of his beautiful 'fiancée', Earth-born playboy Moris Keniston arrives on the mysterious and hostile planet Sovold. Before he can sample its violent lifestyle and bizarre terrain, or combat the amoral whims of its courts (and blue-haired courtesans) he needs to adopt a suitable diguise.

So, with shaved head and skin dyed beige, he dons the yellow-crested helmet and green cloak of a Messenger of the mighty empire of Zhuvastou. Armed only with a heavy sword he is ready to set out on his urgent quest ...

PHILIP JOSE FARMER
Hadon of Ancient Opar

OPAR – the Atlantean colony in the heart of Tarzan's Africa.

OPAR is the setting of this fabulous novel of twelve thousand years ago, when Africa had an inland sea and a mighty civilization bloomed along its forgotten shores, when lost empires flew their time-vanished banners and heroic deeds were commonplace.

Philip José Farmer, chronicler of *Tarzan Alive*, presents here the first great novel of HADON, whose claim to a throne launched him upon an enthralling and dangerous venture.

T. J. Bass

| 413 3467 | The Godwhale | 65p |

Alfred Bester

| 413 3457 | Extro | 60p |

John Brunner

| 413 3458 | The Wrong End of Time | 55p |

Philip K. Dick

413 3654	Dr Futurity	60p
413 3655	The Unteleported Man	50p
413 3653	The Crack in Space	70p
417 0197	The Simulacra	75p

Philip José Farmer

| 417 0100 | Hadon of Ancient Opar | 70p |
| 417 0177 | Flight to Opar | 75p |

Damon Knight

| 417 0220 | Off Centre | 70p |

Andrew J. Offutt

| 417 0190 | Messenger of Zhuvastou | 80p |

Mack Reynolds

| 417 0178 | Galactic Medal of Honour | 75p |

Clifford D. Simak

413 3690	Way Station	65p
413 3768	Time and Again	75p
413 3760	Cemetery World	70p
413 3695	Time is the Simplest Thing	70p
417 0171	A Choice of Gods	70p

These and other Magnum Books are available at your bookshop or newsagent. In case of difficulties orders may be sent to:

Magnum Books
Cash Sales Department
PO Box 11
Falmouth
Cornwall TR10 109EN

Please send cheque or postal order, no currency, for purchase price quoted and allow the following for postage and packing:

UK — 19p for the first book plus 9p per copy for each additional book ordered, to a maximum of 73p.

BFPO & Eire — 19p for the first book plus 9p per copy for the next 6 books, thereafter 3p per book.

Overseas customers — 20p for the first book and 10p per copy for each additional book.

While every effort is made to keep prices low, it is sometimes necessary to increase prices at short notice. Magnum Books reserve the right to show new retail prices on covers which may differ from those previously advertised in the text or elsewhere.